Sugar Creek Gang
The Mystery Cave

Original title:
Mystery at Sugar Creek

Paul Hutchens

MOODY PRESS
CHICAGO

© 1943 by
PAUL HUTCHENS
Moody Press Edition, 1966

ISBN: 0-8024-6961-2

1 2 3 4 5 6 Printing/LC/Year 94 93 92 91 90 89

Printed in the United States of America

1

The things that happened to the Sugar Creek Gang that very dark night when we all went hunting with Circus's dad's big, long-bodied, long-nosed, long-tongued, long-voiced dogs, would make any boy want them to happen all over again, even if some of them were rather spooky and dangerous.

Let me tell you about our hunting trip right this minute—that is, as soon as I get to it. As you probably know, Circus is the name of the acrobat in our gang. His dad's name is Dan Browne, and he makes his living in the wintertime by hunting and trapping—catching animals whose fur is used to keep people warm and to trim hats and collars for women's coats.

Anyway, the Sugar Creek Gang were all invited by Circus's dad to go hunting with him that very Friday night. All of us expected to have a lot of fun, walking along in the shadows and also in the light of the kerosene lanterns through the dark woods, along the creek, listening to the mournful bawling of the hounds on the trail of—well, most anything such as raccoons, possums, and even skunks. We also all hoped we might run into another bear. Remember the one Little Jim killed in one of the other stories about the gang?

Friday night finally came, which is the best night for a boy to be up late, 'cause there isn't any school on Saturday and he can sleep late in the morning if he wants to. And if his parents want him to, which some parents sometimes don't.

Right after chores were done at our farm, which we did in the dark by lantern light like we do in the late fall and winter, the Collins family, which is ours, ate a grand supper of raw-fried potatoes and milk and cheese and cold apple pie and different things. Boy, it was good!

I looked across the table at my baby sister, Charlotte Ann, who was half sitting and half sliding down in her chair. Her eyes were half shut and her little round, brown head was bobbing like a boy's bobber on his fishing line when he is getting a nibble, just before he gets a bite, then all of a kerplunk it goes all the way under and the fun has begun. Just that minute Charlotte Ann's little round, brown head went down a long way, and my grayish-brownish-haired mom who has a very kind face and the same kind of heart, stood up, untied the cord that held Charlotte Ann in the chair, lifted her carefully with her kind hands, and took her into the dark front room to put her into her bassinet, which I knew had a Scottish terrier designed on its side. I felt proud to think that I knew nearly every kind of dog there was in the world, certainly all the different kinds there were in Sugar Creek, which is a very important part of the world. I even knew the dogs by name, but for some reason we had never had a dog in the Collins family.

Well, for a minute Dad and I were alone, and the way he looked at me made me wonder if I had done anything wrong, or maybe if I was *going* to and he was going to tell me *not* to.

"Well, son," he said, looking at me with his big blue eyes which were buried under his big, blackish-reddish, bushy eyebrows. His teeth were shining under his reddish-brownish moustache, though, and when his teeth are shining like that so I can see them, it is kinda like a dog wagging his tail. That meant he liked me and there wasn't going to be any trouble.

Yet trouble can happen mighty quick in a family if there is a boy in it who likes to do what he likes to do, which I did.

"What?" I said.

6

Dad's voice was deep like it always is, like a bullfrog's voice along Sugar Creek at night, as he said, "I'm sorry, Bill to have to announce that—" Dad stopped and looked long at me.

Say, all of a sudden my heart felt like some wicked magician had changed it into a lump of lead. What was he going to announce? I wondered. What was he waiting for and what had I done wrong, or what was I *about* to do that I shouldn't?

Just that minute while Dad's sentence was still hanging like a heavy weight of some kind about to drop on my head, Mom came in from having tucked Charlotte Ann into her bassinet. "I'll fix a nice lunch for you to take along, Bill, in your school lunch pail. Apple pie, warm cocoa, and sandwiches and—"

And my dad who must have been thinking about what he was going to say and not hearing Mom at all, went on with his sentence by saying, "Sorry to have to announce that Dr. Mellon called up this afternoon and said he would be ready for you to get your teeth filled in the morning at eight. I tried to arrange some other time for you, but we had to take that or wait another week, so you'll have to be home and in bed a little after eleven.

"I've made arrangements for Dan to leave you and Little Jim at Old Man Paddler's cabin where Little Jim's daddy will get you. Little Jim's piano lesson is at nine in the morning anyway, so his mother—"

Well, that was that. Little Jim and I couldn't stay out in the woods as late as the rest of the gang.

My heart was not only lead, but hot lead, 'cause I didn't like to go to a dentist and have my teeth filled, and I didn't want to come home till the rest of the gang did.

I felt sad and must have looked sadder.

"What's the matter?" Mom said. "Don't you like apple pie and cocoa and sandwiches?"

I was thinking about a cavity I had in one of my

7

best teeth, and I was thinking about how I would look with a little piece of shining gold in one of my *front* teeth, so I said to Dad, "What kind of filling?"

And Mom said, "Roast beef and salad dressing."

And Dad said, "*Gold* maybe for one and porcelain for the others."

And my mom exclaimed, "*What* in the—" and stopped just as we heard the sound of steps on our front porch and I saw the flashing of a lantern outside the window and heard different kinds of voices at different pitches. I knew the gang was coming.

In a jiffy I was out of my chair and into my red cross-barred mackinaw, with my red corduroy cap pulled on tight. I was making a dive for the door when Dad's deep voice stopped me by saying, "You forgot your manners again."

So I said, "I mean, excuse me, please. Where's my lunch, Mom?" Maybe I didn't have any manners at all for a minute.

Lunch wasn't ready, so I went outside and waited for it and for the rest of the gang to come, our house being their place where they had all agreed to meet first. I say the *rest* of the gang 'cause there were only two there: Poetry, our barrel-shaped member, who knows a hundred and one poems by heart, and Dragonfly, the spindly-legged member whose eyes are too large for his little head and whose nose is crooked at the bottom. Dragonfly's teeth are also too large, and *will* be until his face and head grow some more, and he is always seeing things which are not there—*sometimes* anyway. The very minute I saw Dragonfly with his big dragonfly-like eyes shining in the lantern light, I knew, or anyway I *felt*, that there was going to be something new and different happen on our hunting trip—nothing to *worry* about, of course, but just to *wonder* about. I had enough to worry me by thinking of the dentist and the next morning at eight o'clock.

8

I hadn't any sooner gotten outside than there was a whimpering sound at my knees. Looking down I saw a brown-tan long-muzzled dog with curly rough hair. It was sniffing at my boots to see if it liked me enough to wag its stumpy tail at me, which it did, only it didn't waste much time on me, 'cause right that minute our old black and white cat, whose name is Mixy, came arching her back along the side of the porch, looking for somebody's legs to rub up against. She and that Airedale saw and smelled each other at the same time.

The next thing I knew a streak of brown and a streak of black and white were cutting a terribly fast hole through the dark on the way to our barn.

Dragonfly let out a yell, "Hey, Jeep! Leave that cat alone!"

It was Dragonfly's new dog which his parents had bought for him somewhere.

Just then Poetry's squawky, duck-like voice began quoting one of his poems. It sounded funny and his fat face looked funnier in the light of his lantern which he was holding up close to it to see if he could see what was happening to the cat—or maybe to the dog, 'cause our old Mixy cat was a fierce fighter if a dog ever caught up with her in a race. The poem went like this:

Hey! diddle, diddle,
The cat and the fiddle,
    The cow jumped over the moon.
The little dog laughed
To see such sport,
    And the dish ran away with the spoon.

"The dog ran away with the *cat*, you mean," I said.

Just then we heard a banging noise out in the barnyard which sounded like one of our cows had tried to jump over the moon and hadn't been able to make it on account of the barn or a hog house being in the way.

9

"You *certainly* aren't going to take that Airedale along with us on our hunting trip!" I said to Dragonfly.

"I *certainly* am!" he replied. Then he added, "And why *not*?

It was Poetry who answered squawkily, " 'Cause any dog that is nervous like that and goes shooting like a torpedo after a cat wouldn't be worth a *picayune* on a hunting trip. He'd have the hounds off the trail half the time barking at rabbits in a brushpile, or up the wrong tree, or chasing somebody's house cat."

"What's a *picayune*?" Dragonfly wanted to know, and because I'd had the word in spelling class that week and had looked it up, I said, "A *picayune* is 'a person or a thing of trifling value.' "

Say, that little spindle-legged guy was peeved on account of what Poetry had said about his Airedale, so he said saucily, "Here, Picayune, give me that lantern a minute and I'll go out and save the cat's life." He snatched the lantern which Poetry let him have, and started off to the barn lickety-sizzle, leaving Poetry and me alone in the dark, with the light from our kerosene lamp in the house shining out across the porch on Poetry's green corduroy cap and his brown and light-brown leather jacket. The light also shone on his fat face and his very big feet, he having the longest feet in all the Sugar Creek Gang. He was wearing long leather boots with rubbers on them to keep his feet dry because it was muddy in places and there would be plenty of wet grass and leaves and maybe puddles to walk and run in on our hunting trip. The weather was just right for hunting though, 'cause when the ground is damp like that, the hounds can smell better, and the coons and possums and things leave their scent on the leaves and grass and wherever they walk or run or climb.

I had learned all these things from my dad and especially from Circus himself. Besides, any boy on a farm knows these things.

Just that minute we heard galloping hoofs and a snorting horse. In a jiffy Circus, our acrobat, came riding into our lane and up to our back door. The minute his pony slid to a quick stop and was standing still, Circus put his hands on the saddle, kicked his feet out of the stirrups, and in a split second was standing on his hands with his medium-sized feet balanced in the air for a quick jiffy before he swung himself out over the pony's heaving side and alighted on the board walk beside me and Poetry.

"Hello, Gang," he said. "Where's everybody?"

"I'm right here!" a new voice called from the path that ran through our orchard. Looking around behind me I saw a flashlight bobbing along back and forth like the pendulum on our kitchen clock. It was two people, a tallish boy with his cap on sideways, and a short, short-legged little guy with his cap on backwards and with the bill turned up. It was Big Jim and Little Jim. Big Jim was wearing rubber boots and Little Jim also, and all of us were wearing mittens or gloves.

That was all of the original Sugar Creek Gang except Dragonfly, who just that minute came galloping up from the barn, swinging Poetry's lantern, his Airedale dog all around him and in front of him and behind him at almost the same time. The light of the lantern was making so many shadows in different directions that Dragonfly looked like about three boys with four dogs all around him.

There was one other member of our gang, Little Tom Till, who lived across the creek a half mile or so away, and whose big brother Bob had caused us so much trouble but was a better boy now. Little Tom Till had red hair and freckles like mine and wasn't ashamed of it. He and I didn't have any more fights, 'cause I'd found out he was a better little guy on the *inside* than

11

showed on the *outside*, like lots of red-haired, freckled-faced people are—including maybe me, some of the time.

Just as I was wondering if red-haired Little Tom was coming, Little Jim, who is my best friend in the whole gang except maybe Poetry or Dragonfly, sidled over to me and, tugging at my arm, started to tell me something. I leaned over and listened and he said, "Tom Till's daddy is gone again and nobody knows where. My daddy says we better—we'd better—"

"Anybody seen anything of Tom?" Big Jim wanted to know. Big Jim and Big Bob Till had been terrible enemies for a year or two, you know, but weren't anymore although they still didn't like each other very well and maybe never would. Big Jim, though, was a kind-hearted boy, and he was being especially kind to Little Tom Till.

That question of Big Jim's stopped Little Jim from telling me the rest of what he was about to tell me, until later.

"Tom can't come," Little Jim said.

Then Little Jim tugged at my arm again and I leaned over again and he started to finish his sentence again, and it was, "John Till is in trouble with the police, and Daddy says we'd better—we'd better—"

Just that second our back door swung open wide and the light came splashing out across the porch and into all our faces, and my Mom called, "Your lunch is ready, Bill! Oh, hello, everybody! They're all here, Daddy!" she called back into our house to my dad.

My big, very strong dad came out onto the porch and looked us over with his eyes that were almost buried under his bushy brows, and said, "Well, Gang, have a good time. I'm sorry I can't go along, but I have some letters to write. When you get to Seneth Paddler's cabin up in the hills, tell him I'll be around to see him about Cuba tomorrow some time."

12

"About *who*?" Dragonfly asked.

"Cuba isn't a *who*!" Poetry barked disgustedly. "It's a *what*. Cuba is an island in the West Indies. It's seven hundred miles long and from twenty-five to eighty miles wide. It was discovered by Columbus and is called the Pearl of the Antilles, and Columbus said it was the most beautiful island in the world and—"

"We'd better get going," Circus said. "Dad told me to tell you to hurry up. That's why he sent me over, to tell you all to step on the gas. The hounds are almost crazy to get started, and it may either rain or clear off or turn cold, and if it turns cold and freezes, they can't trail very well."

That was that, and Little Jim still hadn't told me what his dad wanted him to tell me—or us.

In another jiffy we were ready, with Little Jim riding up on the pony with Circus, and the rest of us scrambling along behind the pony, Dragonfly and his crazy Airedale shuffling along all around and in between us. Dad's last words were ringing in my ears, "Don't forget, Bill, to tell Seneth Paddler I'll be over to see him tomorrow about Cuba."

That Cuba business didn't interest us very much except that we all knew that Old Man Paddler, who is one of the grandest old men that ever lived, had probably asked my father to send some money down there to some missionaries, Old Man Paddler being very much interested in things like that.

Just that minute Dragonfly's Airedale darted in between my legs on his awkward way across the road to give chase to a rabbit which had just dashed across, and I stumbled over him and over myself and went down into a small puddle.

"That *crazy* dog!" I exclaimed from somewhere in the center of the road. "What on earth do you want him to go along for?"

"That's what *I* say!" Poetry puffed beside me, and

13

would you believe it? Poetry also was getting up off the ground at the same time I was.

"He's a wonderful dog," Dragonfly said defensively. "Just you wait and see. He'll maybe catch a bear or a lion, or maybe save somebody's life or something. I read a story once about—"

"Hurry *up*, you guys!" Circus called back to us from his pony, and we *did*, all of us starting to run to try to keep up with Circus.

Poetry, puffing along beside me said between puffs, "I just know that curly-haired mongrel is going to get us into trouble."

"He's *not* a mongrel!" Dragonfly exclaimed behind us. "He's a purebred Airedale."

"He's a *picayune!*" I told Dragonfly. "He's a *thing* of trifling value."

"He's a *person!*" Dragonfly cried. "Here, Jeep! Here, Jeep!" he called. "Come back here and leave that rabbit alone! We're going *coon* hunting!"

Pretty soon we came in sight of Circus's kinda oldish looking house where there was a light in an upstairs window with somebody moving about, maybe turning down the covers for some of Circus's many sisters who lived there, he being the only boy.

Circus's dad and Big Jim's dad's hired hand, who lived close by, were there waiting for us with two more kerosene lanterns, and with a long, powerful flashlight and one long rifle. Tied right close to their woodshed were two great big, sad-faced, long-nosed, long-eared, long-bodied hounds, one a rusty red color, and the other a kind of a blue and gray. They were leaping and trembling and acting like wild things, trying to get loose so they could go where they wanted to go.

Circus put his pony away in their barn, came back to where we were, and in less than three minutes we were on our way. Say, Circus's dad, who had on a great big sheep-lined brown coat and high boots, as also did

14

Big Jim's dad's hired man, went over to the dogs, scolded them a jiffy so they would be quiet, and unsnapped their leashes. You should have seen them go, just like two streaks of greased lightning, out across the yard, and over the fence and straight for Sugar Creek. Maybe they must have smelled something out there, and knew just where to go first, for we hadn't all of us been following along behind more than a half minute when one of the dogs whose name was Old Bawler, the gray and blue one, let out a wild, long, sad bawl that sounded like a loon and a woman crying for help and running at the same time:

"*Whooooooooo . . . Whooooooo . . .*"

Then Old Sol, the red and rusty hound took up the cry, and his voice was deep and hollow like it was coming through a long hollow log in a cave, and he was in a lot of trouble:

"*WHOOOOOOOO . . . WHOOOOOOOO . . .*"

"It's a coon!" Circus cried, and so did Circus's dad and almost all of us, each one trying to be first to tell the other one what we thought it was.

"It's headed straight for Sugar Creek! Come on! Everybody!"

And away we went—lanterns, boots, boys, Dragonfly, Jeep and all running, sloshety-crunchety-jump, leap-slippety-sizzle, through the woods, over logs and up and down little hills and around brush piles and briar patches, and panting and feeling fine and excited and wondering if it was a coon or a fox or what.

2

I couldn't help but notice, though, that just a minute or two after we had started, the dogs had changed the direction they were running and were running not toward Sugar Creek but toward the little stream of water which we called the "branch" and which emptied itself into the creek quite a long ways away from where we were.

It looked like they were going to take us right back toward Circus's house again, and we all followed along behind them running or walking, whatever we had to do. Sometimes we had to hurry to keep up with the dogs and then again we had to sort of just amble along at a snail's pace, 'cause the dogs would lose the trail, going around a tree or a brushpile or somewhere.

"What do you know about *that?*" I heard Circus say. "It's going straight for our orchard!" And it looked like it was. It had left the woods. The dogs were away up ahead of us, with Jeep darting in and out and around. First he would be with us, then he would be away up ahead with the real dogs.

Say, pretty soon while we were walking along, I heard little Jeep barking all by himself. He had a funny sort of bark which was entirely different from any he had had yet. It sounded like he felt like he had done something wonderful. He wasn't up there with the other dogs at all. He was over all by himself, barking up a little tree right at the edge of Circus's orchard. In fact, he was barking up a persimmon tree.

The men, as I told you, were away on up ahead of us following the hounds which had already turned aside and started toward Sugar Creek again. Say, do you know what? Circus, Big Jim, Poetry, Dragonfly, Little Jim, and I stopped awhile there to see what Jeep was after, which we supposed was a house cat.

Poetry squawked up then and said, "I'll bet it's one of Circus's sisters, and that picayune doesn't know the difference." Circus had so many sisters but he couldn't help it. For that reason he didn't know how to wipe dishes very well.

I had Big Jim's flashlight, and I shoved its light up toward the top of that tree and around and couldn't see anything. Some of the leaves of the persimmon tree were still on, and were dark-brownish color, not round and oval like they are in the summertime when they are so large and shining and green, but curled up like old Jack Frost had left them.

Then my flashlight showed me, about halfway up, a queer looking little lightish-gray creature of some kind. Jeep was all around that tree at the same time, barking and yelping and jumping up and down, scratching his claws on the thick, scaly brown bark.

Do you know what I saw when my flashlight was focused up there? Right in the crotch of a limb was *something*. The under part of it was very dark. Beginning along about the middle of its side and going up toward its back it was black and white, its fur mixed like a man's hair who is maybe about 47 years old. Its hair was nice and long, or rather its fur. Say, it swung around a little and shut its little eyes against the light, and I could see that its head was a different color, a kinda yellowish-white. Its cheeks were just as white as the snow would be in about another two weeks, or maybe even that very night, if it should happen to snow, which I wished it would.

I knew right away what it was 'cause of its long tail.

"Boy, oh boy!" I heard Poetry say. "It's a possum!"

"Sure!" I heard Little Jim say. "It's a big possum! Look at his little black ears, would ya!"

"Those ears aren't black," Dragonfly said. "Not all

18

black anyway. See that little yellow streak up there on the tiptop of its ears!"

The under part of the possum, as I told you, is dark, and the fur there is also shorter than the other part, with just a few white hairs sprinkled in.

"I don't think it's a possum," Dragonfly went on to say, " 'cause look how black its legs are, and look how black its feet are."

I lowered my voice disgustedly, and said, "It's a possum!"

I held my light on its tail, pushing the light right up close to the possum, until the gray-furred little varmint scrambled around, turned his tail to me and began to climb on up the tree.

"See that tail!" I exclaimed. "That's what they call a prehensile tail!"

Big Jim, who was standing quietly looking on, said, "Here, Bill, let me have that flashlight!"

He had it before I could let loose of it almost, and was shoving it still closer to the possum, reaching as high as he could.

Say, with all that noise going on, with all of us jabbering to each other, and with Jeep barking and yelping, we forgot all about old Bawler with her loon-like voice and Old Sol with his hollow, gruff voice. We forgot all about Circus's dad and Big Jim's dad's hired man. We were so excited because Jeep had already proved that he wasn't such an ignorant dog, although I still claimed that he was a picayune. It had just been an accident that he had caught that possum.

So I said to Dragonfly, "It's just an accident that he ran onto this possum here."

"Yeah," Little Jim said, feeling like teasing somebody himself. "I bet he didn't know the difference when the possum's trail crossed the coon's trail, and he got off on this sidetrack."

"Sure," I said. "He thinks a possum is important."

19

Circus spoke up and said, "It *is* important! That possum is worth two dollars!"

Well, sir, the possum was not interested in having us too close to him, so he squirmed on up the tree, reaching one long front leg after the other from one limb to another, and pretty soon he was going up very fast. I could see his long prehensile tail dragging along behind him. "See his prehensile tail!" I exclaimed.

Dragonfly answered me by saying, "What's a prehensile tail?"

As I told you, I'd been looking up useful words and learning how to use them by using them, so I said, "A prehensile tail is a tail that can hold onto things almost as well as a boy's hand can."

"A possum can hang by its tail as easy," Poetry said to Dragonfly, wanting to tell what he knew too, "—as easy as Circus can hang by his!" Circus, as you know, was our acrobat.

Well, that was a bright remark, and we all had a good laugh.

"*That*," Circus answered gruffly, "is a bright remark without the glow!" I heard a bit of scuffling behind and beside me and looked around just in time to see Poetry beginning to get up off the ground.

Circus decided it was time to go into action. He just swung himself up into the branches of that persimmon tree and started up hand over hand after the possum. It was a funny sight, to see our Circus going up the tree following the possum and to see the possum hurrying and hurrying up ahead of Circus.

In another jiffy Circus, who was still on the way up, called back to us, "It's a good thing we are catching this possum. We've been missing too many chickens out of our chicken house!"

That was a fact too. Possums eat a lot of different things which they shouldn't 'cause they not only eat all kinds of insects in the summertime, but they are very

20

destructive animals. Nearly every bird that nests on the ground around Sugar Creek has to be afraid an old possum will come along and tear up its nest and eat all the little baby birds or destroy the eggs. Not only that, it goes right out into people's chicken yards and chicken houses at night, and if it gets a chance in summer or spring it will eat the *little* chickens too. If it's a big possum, it will catch even the big chickens and kill them and eat them.

I remembered all that while Circus was on his way up the persimmon tree. Once he stopped to pick and eat one of the little plum-sized yellow persimmons, which, since fall and frost had come, were ripe and tasted very good to boys and possums. But in the summer and early fall, they made your lips pucker if you tasted one.

Little Jim, who never liked to see anything get hurt, piped up and said, calling up to Circus, "My dad says that possums are very good to catch the moles too," which is just like Little Jim—always defending something or somebody, which maybe is a very good character trait, anyway.

Big Jim was holding his flashlight on the little gray varmint and Circus, who knew that tree almost by heart and where every limb was 'cause he'd climbed every tree on their place and every one along Sugar Creek almost, didn't have to wonder where the next limb was even if he couldn't see it. He just went right on up that tree.

"I'm going to shake him down!" he called back to us, and he started to do what he said he was going to do.

By that time, the possum was away up close to the top of the persimmon tree and was out on the end of one of the branches, clear out among the twigs.

Circus grabbed hold of the small limb that the possum was on and started to shake it, holding onto the trunk of the tree with one hand and shaking with the other one, as hard as he could. Boy, that possum with

21

his gray hair and his blackish stomach and his very black legs and feet held on tight, I can tell you. He even held on tight with his long, gray, round, tapering, prehensile tail.

Say, Circus knew how to shake possums out of a tree all right. He just jerked and shook and jerked and shook that branch and stopped and shook and jerked, and suddenly the feet of that possum were loose. And would you believe it? Not only his front feet were loose and his back black feet, but every single foot was loose and that clever gray-furred little rascal, that had his eyes shut 'cause he didn't like to look into the flashlight, was hanging by his tail only. His back feet were reaching back and up trying to clasp the limb his tail was still holding onto, like a turtle's legs searching all around trying to get hold of a boy's hand which is holding it up by its tail, and also like a crawfish's pincers do when you have hold of it somewhere. Generally it does find your hand or finger somewhere just before you let go of it and it gets away.

Circus gave another quick, sharp jerk, but the possum just that second managed to get a grip on the limb again, away out where he was, and he scrambled up and onto it.

Big Jim threw up an idea to Circus when he called, "How about it? Maybe your dad wants that persimmon pruned up there a little!"

That was a good idea, so Circus had his knife out right away and decided that that limb wouldn't be needed anymore. It was cut off in almost no time. Circus gave it a little shove, and out went Mr. Possum down through the outer branches of the tree to the ground. The minute it struck it curled itself up into a ball like they say porcupines do when they're about to be caught.

Well, Jeep didn't know what to make of it. He darted in there and started to grab hold of the possum with his teeth. Then he let go and jumped back, and then dived in again and jumbed back, and barked and panted and panted and barked and dived in again.

All the time the possum was still curled up in a ball acting like it was sound asleep.

"He's playing possum," Poetry cried, and that was true. Possums do that, you know, when they're about to be caught. They curl up into a little ball, shut their eyes and open their mouths with a silly sickly grin on their white faces and look like they are dead. Then if you leave them alone, they'll run away.

Picayune darted in again, and this time actually grabbed the possum with his teeth, shook him like he was a big rat, then jumped back like he was almost half scared to death.

You couldn't wake up that possum though. It was lying on its side and had its head down between its forelegs. Its sharp, long nose was clear down almost touching its stomach, like it was trying maybe to protect its head from being hit, or maybe to put its chin down on its breast to keep it from getting bit in the throat, that being the place where a weasel likes to bite first when it catches a live supper.

Dragonfly spoke up then and said, "I wonder if he thinks he's safe just because he has his head down between his two front legs, like an ostrich does when it buries its head in the sand when there is danger."

Poetry answered him by saying with his duck-like voice. "Possums don't think. Possums *can't* think. Animals don't have brains enough to think."

"*Dogs* do," Dragonfly said, and it looked like the argument was in his favor. We didn't have time to have an argument right then, though. Big Jim told them to keep still.

Circus knew exactly what to do with a possum and how to kill it so it would die very quickly without having more than a minute's pain.

23

Little Jim turned his face away while Circus did that. Then Circus took the possum by its prehensile tail and said, grunting a little, "He's pretty heavy to carry all the way. I think I'll lock him up in our woodshed. Come on, everybody!"

We all came on, following him up to their weathered old house where we waited at the gate, all of us boys feeling very bashful on account of Circus having so many sisters. Only one of them would even look at a boy with red hair and freckles. Her name is Lucille, and she isn't afraid of spiders.

Pretty soon Circus was back again, and we all started to holler to each other, "Hurry up or we'll never catch up with them."

Almost as soon as we were out in the woods again, we heard old Bawler's high voice—and it sounded very far away—going "*Whoooooooo . . . !*"

At the same time, or a fraction of a second later, we heard Old Sol's baritone voice also bawling, "*WHOOOOOOO . . . !*"

"I'll bet they've really found a coon's trail!" one of us said to the rest of us, and we ran still faster, getting closer to the men in almost a little while.

"If it *is* a coon," Circus yelled to us, "we'll have a real fight on our hands."

3

It's a queer feeling—running and panting and stopping for breath and hurrying on and climbing over rail fences, and dodging around trees, lickety-splashety-crunchety-sizzle through the woods, not being able to see very far on account of the dark, and with everybody else all around you or in front of you or behind you as excited as you are.

We could hear the bawling of the hounds and also the sharp quick nervous barks of Dragonfly's Airedale, who was also in the coon chase, far ahead of all of us and running with the hounds.

Once when I caught up with Circus's dad and Big Jim's dad's hired man, I heard Circus's dad say, "Any dog that will leave a coon's trail for a possum's can't be trusted."

And that's how we came to find out that the men knew all the time we were catching a possum back there. "We thought we'd let the Sugar Creek Gang have some fun of their own," Circus's dad explained to us. "Besides, we couldn't leave the hounds on a trail like this one is."

Just the same the men wanted to know all about the possum, which we told them, also handing each one of them a ripe persimmon, which some of us had filled our pockets with just before we'd left the tree. They were right about Jeep, though. He simply ran off on every sidetrack there was, always diving off in any direction after a rabbit which would jump up and run.

But we couldn't let that spoil our fun. Boy, oh boy! Bawler with her high pitched voice and Old Sol with his deep gruff voice knew what they were doing, and they stuck to it. Or maybe I should say they kept their noses not more than a few inches from the ground, running this way and that wherever the coon's feet had gone, and it didn't make any difference how many rabbits jumped in front of them. They acted as if a rabbit wasn't any more important to them than a crumb of bread that fell from a hungry boy's roast beef sandwich while he was eating.

Once, when for a while Old Bawler and Old Sol were having trouble finding the coon's trail which they'd lost, Little Jim and I had a very interesting visit, and I found out what he'd tried to tell me about old hook-nosed John Till.

Say, the hounds were worried, trying to untangle the coon's knotty trail. They were jumping over logs and running around trees and splashing across a little stream of water, which is called the branch, splashing back again, whining and complaining and not bawling at all. But they were acting worried like a boy when he is stuck with an arithmetic problem and his dad isn't there to ask helpful questions and maybe give an idea that will give him an idea how to work it.

It was while they were having that trouble that we all sat down and waited beside and *on* a big maple tree which had fallen in a summer storm.

One thing I had always liked to do was to go out into the woods along Sugar Creek, or somewhere where men were cutting wood, and climb up on the fallen trunk of a big tree and walk on it all the way from the base to the very top. Then when I couldn't walk any further 'cause there wasn't any more trunk, I'd climb one of the upright branches at the top end and perch myself in a crotch in a limb and sit and sway back and forth and up and down and imagine myself to be riding on a cloud or in an airplane, or maybe in a boat on an ocean or a lake.

So Little Jim and I, when we saw maybe everybody was going to have to wait a while till the hounds had solved their problem, took Big Jim's flashlight and climbed up on the maple tree trunk and, balancing ourselves, started carefully to walk toward the top maybe a hundred feet away, which was in the opposite direction from the little stream.

" 'Smatter?" Little Jim asked me when we were by ourselves and holding onto each other and to an upright limb to keep from falling off the tree.

"Nothing," I said. "Come on, let's go all the way."

"I mean," Little Jim said, holding onto me with both hands and almost falling off at the same time, "I mean, why can't the dogs find the coon?"

"They've lost the trail," I said. "Old Mr. Raccoon knows we're after him and he doesn't want to be a collar for any woman's coat, so he has maybe jumped out into the water and waded along a while, and his smell has already been carried down in the current. Maybe he's a hundred yards down there himself and will climb out on the other side, or else he'll stay in the water till he gets clear to Sugar Creek, and then he'll find a safe place in a hollow tree and won't get caught."

By the time I'd finished explaining all that to Little Jim, we had already started on up the tree trunk. Soon we were clear to the end and were perched up on one of the branches, swinging back and forth and feeling fine, and as good as if we'd just had our report cards in school and all our grades were A's and B's instead of what some of them sometimes are and shouldn't be.

"Do you know what I wish?" Little Jim asked me, and his voice was wistful, like his mouse-like voice is sometimes. I expected him to say something very important 'cause Little Jim is the only one of the Sugar Creek Gang who has ideas like that all by himself without somebody else thinking of them first. Anyway this is what he said, "I wish—" He stopped and gave his body a big long lurch, and the limb of the tree we were on swayed back and forth, back and forth "—I wish we don't catch up with the coon. I hope it gets away!"

"*What!*" I said. "Why Circus's dad could get maybe nine dollars for it, and that would buy flour and meat and fruit and —"

"Yeah," Little Jim said in a kinda trembly voice. "But just the same, I hope the coon gets away and hope Circus's family has flour and meat and fruit, too."

We rocked a while, back and forth, back and forth, up and down, and I was thinking what if Poetry was with us and the branch was strong enough to hold him, too, he'd probably begin to say in his half-boy-half-man voice,

> Rock-a-bye baby in the tree top,
> When the wind blows, the cradle will rock,
> When the bough breaks—

That was as far as I got to think just then 'cause Little Jim, whose father, as you maybe know, is the township trustee and knows all the important things that go on in the country, said to me, "John Till is running away from the police, and they are on his trail just like Old Bawler and Old Sol are on the coon's trail, and my dad says we'd better—"

Well, I knew I was going to hear what he had to say, and I had already guessed it would be something different from what most any boy would say, on account of Little Jim, as I told you, being the best little guy in the world, and also maybe the best Christian in the whole gang. So I wasn't surprised when he said, finally finishing the sentence he'd started an hour or two before, "We'd better *pray*" (think of it—pray!) "that the Lord won't let him get shot 'cause he's not saved, and if he died he'd be lost forever!"

Right after Little Jim said that, everything was quiet for a while, neither one of us saying anything. I looked away a minute and thought of little red-haired Tom Till who had started to go to Sunday school right

28

after I'd licked him once in a fight and after Little Jim had saved his life by shooting a fierce mad old mother bear that was about to eat him up. And I thought of Bob Till who had had trouble with the police himself, and was on parole now to Little Jim's dad and I thought of Little Tom's sad-faced mother who had to sew and bake and wash hard for the family without enough money to buy things with, all on account of hook-nosed John Till's spending nearly everything he made for beer and stronger drink. And I felt very sad. I guess maybe I did, without taking very much time, *think* a prayer to God Himself that was something like this, "Please do something in the Till family that will help Little Tom's sad mom to be happy."

Then I looked away down the tree trunk through the branches which still had some of their leaves on them to where the men and the rest of the gang were sitting in the shadows of their lanterns and I could hear the splashing of the dogs in the stream, in and out, and I could hear them whimpering and their noses sniffling anxiously and I could hear a very quiet wind sighing in the trees above us and I felt sad inside, and at the same time I felt kinda white, like a little warm light was shining there 'cause maybe it does a boy good to pray for somebody besides himself.

Just that minute, I heard a high, long-voiced bawl far up the branch. It was Old Bawler, who had found the trail again and was running in another direction. Then Old Sol's voice rolled out in a deep mournful sound, and the chase was on again. It wasn't until after Little Jim and I had unscrambled ourselves from where we were, all tangled up in the tree crotch and each other, and were following along with the rest of the hunters and also with Jeep, the picayune, that I realized that Little Jim had said something else and it was, "Do you know what I just prayed? I prayed that if John Till had to get shot *first*, before he would repent of his sins,

29

that God would let the police *shoot* him, but *not* kill him!"

Imagine that little guy praying a prayer like that!

While we were splashing along again on the chase, following the dogs, swinging our lanterns and flashlights and feeling fine, and I wishing the time wasn't going so fast toward eleven o'clock, and wishing I didn't have to go to the dentist tomorrow morning, I began to feel queer in my heart, as if maybe Little Jim had prayed something very important. Maybe he was right. Maybe if John Till had a lot of trouble and maybe if he got scared terribly bad, he'd think about things and about how mean he was to his wife and boys and how selfish he was in spending all the money on himself and his appetite for drink. And maybe he'd—well, as Little Jim said—maybe he would *repent*, which means to really be sorry for sin, enough, as my dad and mom have taught me, to actually *confess* it to God and be forgiven and saved so as never to drink again.

Then I got to wishing that if something *had* to happen to John Till before he'd wake up, if he didn't have sense enough to repent without being *made* to, whatever was going to happen to him would happen mighty quick for the sake of his sad-faced wife and his boys which needed the right kind of a dad as well as the right kind of a mom.

I even wished that something would happen that very night while he was running away from the police which were on his trail, like hounds on an animal's trail, John Till being so mean that he was almost even worse than an animal—certainly worse than a possum or a coon which doesn't know any better. Old hook-nosed John Till did know better, I thought.

Just that second I heard a shot from somewhere, and I knew it wasn't from any of us.

Dragonfly who was in front of me stopped dead still in his tracks and I bumped squarely into him and into

30

his dog which right that minute was there also. "What was that?" Dragonfly asked.

Poetry, who was puffing along behind me, bumped into me and said, "That? That was probably an automobile backfiring. That's a road over there. Somebody's car probably had to slow down for Sugar Creek bridge, and then when it started again, it backfired."

4

We didn't get to think any longer about whether hook-nosed John Till had been shot. Anyway just that minute the dogs, including the little Airedale which belonged to Dragonfly, started making more noise than ever as if the trail was getting what is called "hot." That meant the dogs were getting closer and closer to the coon and might catch up with it any minute.

In fact that was what I heard Circus say, Circus being just ahead of me—"Listen to that, would you? Hear Old Bawler bawl? The trail is getting hot!"

And so were all of us, from running so fast and even faster, down along the little stream toward its mouth, which is the place where it emptied itself into Sugar Creek, and where Dragonfly and I once caught a very large black bass.

We were hurrying, splashety-sizzlety, all around logs and over logs and all around the little stream, which we called a "branch," meaning it was a tributary stream, which any boy who studies geography knows about.

Because, as I told you, I was trying to learn a lot of new words and how to use them by using them, I said to Poetry who on nearly every chase had a hard time to keep up with the rest of us, and was puffing along behind me—I said over my shoulder to him—"I hope the coon doesn't dive into the tributary again and lose his scent."

And Poetry, trying to be funny and not being, puffed out into my ear, "Raccoons don't have any sense when dogs are after them."

Dragonfly, whose spindly legs were working terribly fast right along the other side of me, also tried to be funny, and wasn't, when he yelled across to the rest of us, "They may not have many dollars and cents but they can sense danger when they know dogs are after them,"—which goes to show that even though we were excited, we were having fun.

Old Sol with his deep voice which sounded like it was coming through a long hollow log in a cave, was going like this, "*WHOOOO . . . ! WHOOOO!*"

Old Bawler, whose voice was high pitched like a loon's and like a woman's screaming voice in a haunted house, sounded like this, "*Whoooooooooo . . . ! Whooooo-ooo!*"

"Hey!" Somebody's voice behind us called, "Wait for me!" It was Little Jim whose short legs couldn't work fast enough for him to keep up with us. All of us stopped except Big Jim and the men and waited till Little Jim whizzed up to us. Then Poetry asked him, "Say, Little Jim, you know all about music. What key are those hounds barking in?" He held his lantern up so I could see Little Jim's kinda half-happy and half-sad face and also see his cap which was still on backwards with its bill turned up.

Little Jim panted a minute and listened before answering, then he said, "They're *both* in the *same* key, I think."

He really was a good musician, you know, his mom being the very best in Sugar Creek township and playing the piano in our church. Little Jim practiced hard every day which is the way to learn anything anyway.

We all kept still a jiffy while Little Jim acted like he was thinking, which he was, and listening. Then he used his own voice and struck the pitch Old Sol's voice had been striking and *was* striking right that minute far down the branch. Then his voice jumped away up high to another pitch, like a bird springing up to a higher rung on a ladder, and he struck the same pitch as Old Bawler was also striking every few seconds.

"*WHOOOOOOO . . . !*" That was like Old Sol.

34

"*Whoooooooo!*" And that was like Old Bawler.

Then that short-legged little guy grinned and said, "Old Sol is on re in the key of F, and Old bawler is on la in the same key!"

I could see that Little Jim was more interested in the chase after that 'cause he could think about the music in the dog's voices. And if there was anything he liked better than anything else, it was music—unless maybe it was some of the sassafras tea which Old Man Paddler used to make for us when we went up to his cabin to see him.

We started to go on when Dragonfly piped up from around us somewhere and asked, "What pitch is Jeep on?" meaning his Airedale.

Well, Jeep was barking like he always had been, every now and then, short and nervous. Little Jim made us all keep quiet a jiffy and then he said, after barking a little himself, imitating the picayune, "He's— Say. He's *off key!*" There was a mischievous grin on his small face. "He's almost hitting fa, but he's sharp."

"See *there!*" Dragonfly exclaimed to me and to the rest of us. "What did I tell you? I knew he was smart. Little Jim says he is," Dragonfly never being very good in his music classes, not knowing *sharp* doesn't mean *smart*.

"I know what key your picayune is barking in," Poetry's squawky voice said in a very low key, and he winked at me.

"You do not!" Dragonfly said, angry at Poetry for calling his dog a picayune.

"I certainly do," Poetry said saucily.

"All right, Smarty, what key is he barking in?"

Poetry winked at me again, and started to run toward where all the dogs were all making more noise than ever. And he tossed his supposed-to-be-funny sentence over his fat shoulder at Dragonfly, and it was, "Your Airedale is barking in the *donkey!*"

35

After that, the rest of us had a hard time keeping up with Dragonfly and Poetry. But Dragonfly was a pretty good sport and even though he was mad, he could see that it was funny. So when he finally caught up with Poetry, instead of socking him, he only said, he knowing a *little* about music though not enough to get good grades in school, "Anyway, *you're* a shaped note and a round note at the same time." And if you know anything about music yourself you'll know that Dragonfly was a pretty smart little spindle-legged guy to think up a joke like that himself.

Say! Things must have been happening up ahead of us where the dogs were and where the chase was hot and getting hotter 'cause all of a sudden, while my thoughts were all tangled up with music and notes and Little Jim and his mom and different music keys and pitches and I was seeing in my mind's eye a keyboard on an organ or piano, those dogs' voices all at once sounded like a pipe organ in a church with somebody *not* playing, but—well, like a *kitten* walking back and forth, back and forth across the black and white keys, like our old Mixy cat, in fact, doing it across the keys of the organ in our own front room at home.

It was a very interesting half-dream I was having while being very wide awake, when things suddenly changed. That is, the dogs changed their tunes and their keys. All three of them were barking like Picayune himself, all of them in short sharp, nervous and excited, *very much* excited voices. Picayune's voice sounded like he was not only excited but like he had done something wonderful and wanted us all to hurry up and come and see. In fact, they all sounded like that.

"Treed!" Circus cried beside me.

"Treed!" I heard Circus's dad yell up ahead of us.

"Treed!" we all called at almost the same time.

"What's *treed* mean?" Dragonfly wanted to know, but nobody answered him.

36

"What's *treed* mean?" Dragonfly asked again, and Little Jim piped across to him and said, "It means the coon has run up a tree to keep from getting caught on the ground just like a possum does," and that was right. Coons do that just like our Mixy cat does sometimes when a dog is after her. She goes like a bullet up a telephone pole or a tree or up our grape-arbor pole to get away.

Say, we all ran as fast and even faster than we could, every one of us, getting in and out of each other's way, until pretty soon I could see what we were all seeing at the same time. There was a big, round, tall maple tree, and around its base were the dogs, barking (not bawling at all) but barking in those same excited staccato barks. I knew that *staccato* was the right musical word for it 'cause just that minute Little Jim said, "Hear them! They're barking staccato now!"

And they were. Old Sol's deep, gruff voice sounded like he had crawled all the way through his hollow log and was very happy about it. Old Bawler's high-pitched, quavering voice sounded like she wasn't scared anymore. And Jeep sounded like he knew he had been right all the time, and had just found it out for sure and was bragging about it.

I tell you there was some excitement going on around there for a minute or two. The three dogs were jumping up and down, up and down, up and down, like hot popcorn in a hot skillet. Then the three would stop barking for a second and just sit and look up, with their tongues hanging out and panting and looking at us to see what we were going to do about things. Then when one of them would bark, the other would, and also the other, and also all of them, and it looked like business.

It looked as if there was certainly something up that tree all right. Pretty soon I saw Big Jim's dad's hired man snap on his very long nickel-plated flashlight and shoot a beam of light away up into the tree. He moved the bright, white, round light it made all around through the leafless branches of that maple tree, back and forth and around and around, making me think of a boy in our schoolhouse with an eraser, moving it across the blackboard to erase the white chalk marks. Only the light of the flashlight was erasing the *dark* off the blackboard of the sky. We could see every gray branch and twig of that tall old maple.

Suddenly beside me I realized that Circus's dad had his rifle ready, and I *knew* that in the next minute or two something was going to happen. I could *feel* it. The flashlight had stopped moving around and was shining on something dark. I realized it wasn't any squirrel's nest of dry leaves either. I knew it for sure when I saw it with my own eyes, then Circus saw it, then Dragonfly saw it, being a little late for a change. Then all of the rest of us saw it, just as plain as day—two little greenish-white, also yellowish, balls of fire away up in the top of the tree, and I knew we'd treed a coon.

We certainly *had* found a coon. You know the very minute Circus's dad raised his long-barreled rifle toward the sky and pointed it directly toward those two green marble-sized balls of fire that seemed to be boring their way into my very mind—I say the very minute that gun was pointed up, all three of the dogs stopped barking, stopped yelping, stopped even whimpering, and were tense, waiting for the sudden explosion that would mean the shell had been fired.

Well, I guess the dogs weren't any more excited than the Sugar Creek Gang was. We were waiting for the shot to be fired too. And all the time I was thinking about the coon, wondering what the coon was *thinking* about, or if it was wondering how it would feel to be shot. I remembered what I'd said to Little Jim not very far back along the trail, which was that the coon probably didn't *want* to be a collar for any woman's coat. Just that minute there was a sound of Circus's dad cocking his rifle, and then a half-jiffy of tense, careful aim right straight toward the two green eyes which I was also seeing. And there was a loud explosion which wasn't maybe so loud but seemed like it 'cause everything else was so quiet. It was like a firecracker which a boy sets off on the Fourth of July.

Then those two green eyes disappeared. The dogs who had been sitting on their haunches looking up with every nerve tense all of a sudden whimpered and kept on trembling and waiting to see what would happen. The next thing I knew there was a crashing among the branches up there.

Then there was a sound of more crashing and still more. And down through the branches of that thousand-limbed giant old maple tree came a great big, round, brownish-gray object that for a jiffy looked like it was half big enough to be a big bear. And then it stopped falling 'cause it must have caught hold of a limb or something and held on.

Big Jim's dad's hired man's flashlight was shining right square on it, and I got my first glimpse of a wild coon when it is scared and mad at the same time. It had large ears that were as large as Mixy's. Its face was lighter than its furry grayish-brown body, and I could see the whitish marking on its scared face. Its nose was pointed, and its stomach was light colored. Above its eyes it was a dark white color and below them it was a light black. Just for a minute I had that glimpse of its face, then it tried to scramble back up the tree, and that's when I got a good look at its tail. Poetry who is good in oral problems in arithmetic said, "Oh boy! *Look!* It's got—one, two, three, four, five, six, seven, rings on its tail!" Of course he couldn't have seen them that fast.

Rings on a coon's tail if you've never seen them, are black fur rings which run all around its tail. The tail, except for the rings, would be all a pale yellow-gray-brown color, like the coon itself.

39

I wondered if it had been shot. Then I knew maybe it *had* been, 'cause it seemed to lose its grip on the limb. It slipped and came down the tree trunk to the ground right in the middle of the excitement of the barking dogs and jabbering boys and scolding men who were scolding the dogs fiercely to keep them from leaping in and tearing the coon's beautiful fur to shreds so it wouldn't be worth a cent to a furrier.

But you can't always get a boy or a dog to obey you right on the second so those three dogs, including Picayune, leaped into the fight. But old Mr. Coon—or *Mrs.* Coon, whichever it was—certainly was very much alive. She backed herself up against that tree and scratched out with both front feet like old Mixy does when she's mad. She hissed and spit and bit. She snapped at the dogs, and the next thing I knew I saw one of Old Bawler's dark, gray-blue ears was split on its end and was bleeding. Evidently the coon had caught her ear in its teeth, and Old Bawler jerking away had had her ear split.

I tell you, the fight was on for good. There was a lot of noise—very, very *fast* noise—of men and boys shouting to each other and to the dogs and differently pitched and very excited dog voices barking at the coon and at the excitement.

But a fight like that never lasts very long. Anyway, this one didn't 'cause something happened that Circus's dad said hardly ever happens. That crazy coon—or wise, I don't know which—did something that only one out of a hundred coons ever do. It all of a sudden curled up into a kind of a ball, just like a possum—just like the possum we had already caught had done—and pretended to be asleep, or dead, maybe waiting for us all to leave it alone a jiffy. Then it would run lickety-sizzle to get some place and get away.

Say, those dogs were surprised. They backed away a second and stood looking down at that silent bunch of

40

gray-brown fur and panted with their tongues hanging out of the side to their mouths. Little spittle ran out of their mouths, and their sides heaved very fast. Then Circus's dad and the hired man scolded them hard, and they obeyed them for a minute.

"Aw shucks!" Poetry said beside me. "It's another possum!"

"It is not!" Circus himself said. "It's just pretending to be dead."

And it was.

Circus's dad had his dogs trained pretty well, or they would have spoiled the fur. But he used his fiercest, very gruff voice on them, and they stopped and slunk back behind him like they'd been licked, like dogs do when they feel sad. Circus's dad then caught them by their collars and they behaved themselves, although they were like race horses waiting a chance to dive in there and make short work of that coon. But it isn't any fun fighting somebody that won't fight.

Anyway, the rest of what happened right then isn't very interesting, only sad. Little Jim looked away, and I even did myself 'cause I didn't want to see the coon be killed. Afterward, when we were all sitting in the shelter of a bluff with a nice friendly fire crackling and the flames leaping up toward the black sky, I sat beside Little Jim on a dry log which we'd found under a ledge and watched the men skin the coon. I felt sad inside, and at the same time I remembered that Circus's family would have some money to spend for food and clothes and things they needed.

Little Jim caught my arm again like he always does when he wants to tell me something, so I leaned over to him and this is what he said, "There's a verse in the Bible which tells about after Adam and Eve had sinned that the Lord Himself made coats of skins and clothed them."

I remembered reading about that in my Bible

41

storybook, but I had forgotten it.

Dragonfly, who was sitting on a knot on the log on the other side of me, said, "What made Him do that? Didn't Adam and Eve have any other clothes?"

I'd never thought about that, so I said, "I don't know."

Poetry, who had been listening and whose parents studied the Bible a lot, said, "If He dressed them in coats of skins, then some animal had to be killed."

I sat there thinking, watching the fire with its long, hurrying flames, and the sparks that were shooting up like yellow raindrops falling up instead of down. I watched the men skin the coon and wondered why animals had to be killed at all and why anybody had to have pain and such things a toothaches, why there were such things as dentists in the world who wanted to fill people's teeth on Saturday morning at eight o'clock.

Thinking of the dentist and of my teeth reminded me of my lunch, which I'd managed to carry all that time without eating any of it and without dropping it, and I was very hungry.

Pretty soon the coon was skinned, and its beautiful fur pelt was folded into Dan Browne's big pocket of his hunting coat. Say, do you know what? All of a jiffy, Dan Browne, who as you know is Circus's dad, said to all of us, "And now, boys, we are ready for the surprise—or *are* you ready?"

Say! That very word *surprise* was one I had always liked. I was in for whatever was coming next. I was also hungry. Then Dan Browne picked up the carcass of the coon, which was all red, and walked over to the fire with it. "Anybody hungry?" he asked.

What? I thought. *He isn't going to cook—!*

I was wrong, though, in what I had been thinking. Say, I saw something then that made me like Circus's dad a lot better. Do you know what? He stood there by the fire only a half-jiffy. Then he turned and walked over to a little, bare, wild rose bush, which in the summertime would have beautiful red roses on it, and I watched him.

He stood there with his back to us and I could hear him sort of mumble, "Little old coon, I'm sorry, but you really *had* been eating too many of our chickens. Thank you, anyway, for your nice warm fur, which I've taken away from you. It will help me support my large family. . . ."

I couldn't hear anymore just then. But when I saw that great big strong man lay the coon's body beside the rosebush and turn around, I knew that he was a kind person. There wasn't any smile on his face for a minute.

Then he turned away quick, and called out to all of us, "Everybody ready?"

We all were, and said so.

"Follow me," Dan Browne said, "and I'll show you."

I tell you I could hardly wait to see what the surprise was going to be.

5

I say I could hardly wait to see what the surprise was. I was always having a hard time waiting for things to happen when I wanted them to happen right away. It wasn't very long, though, until all of us were walking along happily through the woods, following Sugar Creek, going along the path that leads toward the old sycamore tree. You remember that a lot of important things had happened around that old sycamore tree. You remember that while the Sugar Creek Gang had been away on a trip by airplane to Chicago there had been a very bad electric storm. We were up in the plane at the time, riding above the storm on our way to Chicago. When we came back from our trip and were playing around in the woods one sunny afternoon, Dragonfly, who is always seeing things first, had seen a great big, ragged, jagged hole in the side of the hill right at the roots of the old sycamore tree.

Say, do you know what? The lightning had struck that tree and had ripped its way right down the trunk, leaving a big, long, ugly, white-splintered gash all the way down to the roots and into the ground and it had opened up a cave there. Well, you know the rest of that story, how that we went into the mouth of that cave and found that it was shaped something like the inside of the mouth of a large catfish. You maybe remember also, if you've read *The Secret Hideout,* that one dark night we saw a ghost or something there.

Anyway, that cave turned out to be a very long one. There was a rock in its mouth that was a hidden door, and when it was moved we had seen a big black opening into the hill which looked like maybe it didn't have any end at all.

We all went inside that cave, you know— Say, wait

a minute! That's another story which I've already written, and I want to tell you now about what happened when we, all of us, including Jeep, the picayune, went inside.

Well, here we go. Pretty soon we were up there beside the base of the sycamore tree, not very far from the famous Sugar Creek swamp, looking at a big canvas curtain which was hanging in front of the cave's entrance.

"Looks like somebody's been here," Dragonfly said to me.

Somebody had and there was an envelope pinned onto the curtain. Everybody stopped a minute, and Big Jim, being the leader of our gang, was delegated to see what the envelope had in it. He stood there with all our eyes fastened on him, unpinned the envelope which was waterproof and had on the outside, TO THE SUGAR CREEK GANG.

"Go ahead and read it!" Circus's dad said. Big Jim opened the envelope and, with me holding a flashlight for him so he could see, he read. While he was reading I watched the downy fuzz on his upper lip, noticing that it was on again. I remembered he had just shaved it off less than two months before.

"Read it out loud," Dan Browne said, and Big Jim did. His half-man's voice said:

"Members of the Sugar Creek Gang: Attention! A special Sassafras tea party has been planned for you tonight at the nest. Come in the back way!"

The note, I noticed when I looked over Big Jim's elbow, was written in Old Man Paddler's trembling handwriting, and he had signed his name, "Seneth Paddler."

"WHOO*PEE!*" Poetry cried, he being always hungry and always in for a good time. We all felt the same way. We could hardly wait till we got inside that cave and were on our way along its narrow passageway

46

up to Old Man Paddler's cabin.

Well, pretty soon we were all ready to go in. We had our lanterns and flashlights, which would make it easy for us to see. In a jiffy we were inside the catfish-shaped mouth looking through the small hole where the big stone had used to be. The inside was lined with rocks as far back as we could see.

We started moving along, Indian style, which is one at a time, it being too narrow most of the way for two of us to walk beside each other. Poetry, all by himself, had a hard time getting through one narrow place. The dogs were following along behind with strange expressions on their faces as if they didn't know what in the world was happening and were going to follow us to see if it was safe. Jeep was acting kinda scared, because maybe he'd never been in a cave before in all his dog life. I noticed that each dog had on a leather collar with a brass plate with COUNTY DOG LICENSE printed on it, and also a number. Nobody in Sugar Creek County could have a dog and keep him without a license. If any dog was found running loose without a license it could be picked up by an officer and put into a dog jail, which is called a dog pound. And unless somebody came and claimed it and paid for a license for it, that would be the end of that dog.

Well, we were walking along, walking along, walking along. There was gravel and sand covering the solid rock floor. Now and then we had to stoop low to get under a low place. Once we had to squeeze through a very narrow place between two rocks that jutted out.

All this time, though, in spite of the surprise, I kept remembering that I was supposed to *stay* at Old Man Paddler's cabin when we got there. Anyway, I had to be there at eleven o'clock, whether the night of hunting was over or not. It wasn't anywhere near eleven yet, though, so I joined in and had a good time.

Picayune stayed so close to Dragonfly, like he was

afraid, that it reminded Poetry of a poem by Robert Louis Stevenson, and it was:

I have a little shadow that goes in and out with me,
And what can be the use of him is more than I can
see.
He is very, very like me from my heels up to my
head;
And I see him jump before me as I jump into my
bed.

Then Poetry in a mischievous mood started all over again, so Dragonfly could hear him, and said:

I have a little picayune that goes in and out with
me,
And what can be the use of him is more than I can
see.
He is very, very like me from my heels up to my
head—

And that was the end of the poem, on account of Dragonfly and Poetry getting into a scuffle.

We kept on walking along, everybody feeling fine, until pretty soon we came to a heavy wooden door.

Big Jim, our leader, knocked on the door while we waited. None of us were scared 'cause we'd been there before. I was thinking of that kind old man who liked boys so well and knew how to make them happy and how to make them better—rather, he knew how to make a boy *want* to be a better boy.

Just that minute I felt something tugging at my arm, and it was Little Jim again wanting to tell me something. I leaned down and listened. Say, do you know what that little, short-legged guy with his little mouse-like voice said? All this time he must have been thinking about that coon back there and of the story in the Bible about Adam and Eve and how God had put coats of skins on them. Do you know what he said? He said, "Say, Bill! When we get up into Old Man Paddler's cabin and are all sitting around his fireplace drinking sassafras tea and eating lunch, do you care if I ask him to tell us—?" He stopped and waited a minute.

"Ask him to tell us what?" I said, looking down into Little Jim's little face, while Big Jim was knocking again on the wooden door, trying to make somebody in the house hear us.

Little Jim finished his sentence, and it was, "Do you care if I ask Old Man Paddler why Adam and Eve had to have clothes made out of the skins of an animal?"

Just then we heard a sound like somebody was coming down a stairway, and then a trembling, old, kind voice asking, "Who's there?"

Big Jim called through the door, "It's the Sugar Creek Gang!"

Say, those very words sent a thrill all through me. I liked the Sugar Creek Gang so well and was so proud to be a member of such a grand gang of boys, even if I wasn't so very much myself.

It seemed all the time while I was waiting for the trembling old man's voice to answer and for him to open the door that I was trying to remember something, something I was supposed to do or say, or something. *"What is it?"* I asked myself.

I searched every corner of my mind, but I couldn't remember.

Then I heard a sound on the other side of the door, like a steel bar was being slid out of its place. I heard the turning of the handle of a door knob, the sliding of a bolt. The big oak door swung open and there we were, all of us looking into the cellar of that kind old man's cabin.

It didn't take us long to get inside and up the wooden, homemade stairway and inside the warm

49

cabin where there was a roaring fire in the fireplace, hot water on the little wood-burning stove, with the teakettle singing and steam streaming out its spout. Big Jim put the trapdoor down again, and we all sat on chairs or on the floor, wherever we wanted to.

I guess I never realized how cold I was until I got inside that warm cabin and felt the heat on my face and hands. Dragonfly was sitting beside me on the other half of a cane-bottomed chair. The fire was crackling and making a very friendly noise. The fire and the singing teakettle were almost like music. I looked down at Little Jim who was sitting close to Big Jim who was leaning up against a log of wood beside the fireplace, and he was listening to the teakettle and the fire, and also watching the fire as its little hungry flames ate up the logs. Everybody was talking to everybody with nobody listening to the rest of us, like the women of our church do sometimes who come to our house to sew for somebody or just to sew.

I didn't have much of a chance to get in any of the words *I* wanted to say, so I just looked around the room a little at the different things. On the stove beside the teakettle was a steaming large kettle with some red wooden roots of the sassafras shrub in it, which grew in special places along Sugar Creek. The hot water was already red, and I knew the tea was all ready for us to drink—had been for a long time.

I looked all around at all of us. Remembering that Old Man Paddler had named his cabin "The Nest," a brand new name which he'd just lately decided to give it, I got to thinking about all of us crowded into that one room, sitting or lying down in every direction. We were a strange looking nestful of birds, all right: Poetry with his barrel-shaped body in its light-brown leather jacket, with his green corduroy cap still on and his long feet at the lower end of his high leather boots with rubbers on them. There, right beside me—too close to me, in fact,

50

for me not to have to hold onto the back of the chair with my right hand to keep from falling off—was Dragonfly with his spindling legs and his crooked nose which I could see as plain as day in the mirror above the table right in front of me. He was grinning all around at things and his two big incisors were shining, reminding me of eight o'clock tomorrow morning. There was also Little Jim with his cap off: he always remembering to do that when he was in a house, without being told to. There were mittens of different sizes and kinds lying all around everywhere—sixteen of them, in fact—and with Circus's dad and Big Jim's dad's hired man and Old Man Paddler himself we certainly made a crowded nestful of hungry birds.

Some of the other things I saw as I looked around were very different. On the wall above Old Man Paddler's clean-looking bed at the farther end of the cabin near the narrow stairs that led up to a loft, where I had never been but wished I could go sometime, was an ancient flintlock with a very long barrel—the kind of gun they used to use in the days when America had its Civil War and the slaves were freed. Hanging along beside it was a cow's horn, called a powder horn, which was what they used it for.

Hanging on another wall, just above a battery-type radio, was a large rectangular map of the whole world. It was all spread out and tacked up with thumbtacks to the wooden wall. Old Man Paddler had little bright colored pins with large heads of different colors stuck into the map in different places. There were pins in China and Japan—yellow pins; red pins in some parts of South America; pins with black heads on them on some parts of Africa; pins with brown heads in other places, such as in Mexico and Brazil and in some of the islands just below Florida. On a little island named Haiti were *black* pins. On the long caterpillar-shaped map of Cuba were several light-brown pins.

Say, the very minute I saw the name "Cuba" I remembered what I was supposed to remember to tell Old Man Paddler—I was supposed to say what my dad had told me to say, and that was, "Be sure to tell Old Man Paddler that I'll come up to see him tomorrow about Cuba."

Well, I was waiting for a chance to say something, not saying it right away because everybody was still talking to everybody else and nobody was still listening to the rest of us.

Maybe I ought to tell you that almost right away Old Man Paddler started in pouring the tea for us. He'd had it already made, as I told you, and it was steaming on the stove beside the teakettle, a nice red-colored tea which we all liked very much, especially Little Jim. On the table was a big bowl of sugar and cups and cups and cups, enough for the whole Sugar Creek Gang and also for the dogs, and for the rest of us. I forgot to say that the dogs were lying on the floor, very sleepy, just dozing with their eyes half closed, half open. So sleepy and drowsy maybe because they had been working so hard out in the cold. Like some of the farmers who came to the Sugar Creek Church in the wintertime, after being outdoors all week in the cold, they just go to sleep in church almost as soon as our minister starts preaching. It isn't his fault 'cause he always preaches a good sermon which he has worked hard to prepare.

Anyway, the dogs were lying there almost asleep, beside and in front of that warm, friendly fireplace. A minute later the tea was all poured, the sugar was in, and everyone of us were sitting there or half lying down or half sitting up. Some of us were at the table, the rest of us were just holding our cups and saucers on our laps or wherever we wanted to, 'cause it was what is called an informal tea party. There were cookies and cakes also. I was pretty sure Old Man Paddler hadn't baked those cookies 'cause I remembered having seen some exactly like them in our cookie jar back home, and didn't get to take any 'cause Mom had seen me starting to do it, and had said, "Bill Collins! Always ask me first, whether you can have a cookie 'cause I might need them for company." As good a boy as I was, I always had to worry about whether there would be enough cookies for company.

I always hated to ask, even though I knew that if I didn't ask *too* often, I could nearly always have one, or even two.

It wasn't very much of a party but it was certainly a friendly place to be. That kind, old, white-whiskered man with his twinkling, gray-green eyes and his very thick-lensed glasses was the jolliest old man you ever saw. I used to wonder why he was so happy 'cause I'd seen some old men who were very crabby. I guess something I heard my dad say once was right, and that was "The devil doesn't have any happy old men."

I looked at Old Man Paddler, and I knew the devil certainly didn't have him and never would have 'cause God had got him first, and Old Man Paddler had liked being a Christian so well that he'd rather die than not be Jesus' friend.

But it didn't take more than half a jiffy for me to think that. Little Jim was looking at me again. He reached out with the toe of his boot and touched the heel of mine, and I knew that he was getting ready to ask that kind, long-whiskered old man an important question.

I nodded my head to Little Jim to let him know I was ready and that it was the best time, 'cause right that minute everybody was talking about the coon and Circus's dad was just taking the beautiful gray pelt with the seven black furry rings on its tail out of the pocket of his coat which he'd hung up on a homemade wooden costumer near the door when he came in. He was just displaying it there, showing Old Man Paddler what a beautiful thing it was, and we were looking at it and remembering the chase and the fight at the tree, and the shot and everything. The kind old man was admiring it with his gray-green eyes. Suddenly, he said, "Say, that reminds me of a story about Old Tom, the trapper." And before I knew it Old Man Paddler had launched into a story, his bobbing whiskers and his trembling old voice making Little Jim smile all over 'cause he was very fond of that friendly person. In fact it looked as if Seneth Paddler had planned from the very first to tell that story, as if Circus's dad had asked him to tell it so the Sugar Creek Gang could have a very happy time on their hunting trip.

Anyway it was a story which I won't have time to tell now, but it was about Old Tom, the trapper, who was shot through the heart by the Indians one morning when he was running his trapline—shot right through the heart with an Indian arrow. Old Tom had lived along Sugar Creek away back yonder in the days when Seneth Paddler and his twin brother were little boys. Do you know what? Sometime I'm going to have Old Man Paddler tell that story all over again to the Sugar Creek Gang, and I'll write it down when he tells it, or anyway just *like* he tells it if I can, and write it for you in a book maybe.

As soon as the thrilling story was finished, Little Jim's boot touched mine again and he was just ready to ask his question when Circus's dad looked at his heavy watch and then at the gray-blue hound and said, "Well, Bawler, let's go get 'em!"

Talk about a dog waking up in a hurry. I wish I'd get that wide awake that quick when my dad calls me in the morning to wake up and get up—unless it is Saturday morning and there is a tooth to be filled. Say, Old Bawler didn't even take time to stretch like most dogs do when they get up, and yawn and make a queer little noise in their throats. Bawler was up on four feet quicker that Circus can climb a sapling and was over at the front door of the cabin whimpering and scratching and looking back up at Dan Browne and in very good dog language seemed to be saying, "Well, what on earth are we waiting for? Why don't we go *now!*"

Then Dan Browne said, "Sol! Wake up!"

Old rusty-red Sol, whose voice out in the woods is deep and gruff and hollow, let out a kind of low, high whimper, slowly opened his red-brown eyes, looked lazily up at Circus's dad and wagged his long tail a slow, lazy wag and shut his eyes again. I suddenly was reminded of a boy who had a rusty-red head of hair who sometimes does that same thing, and I decided I liked Old Sol better than I did Old Bawler.

Anyway, the men and Circus and Big Jim got up noisily, took their coats and the lanterns and the mittens or gloves whichever they'd had, and we watched them go down the path from Old Man Paddler's door, that leads past his spring and his woodshed. It wasn't too cold to leave the door open a minute, so the four of us youngest boys stood there watching the swinging lanterns and the shadows bouncing around in every direction. Jeep was begging to go, trembling with excitement and sitting down on his haunches beside the doorstep and looking up at Dragonfly for permission.

It didn't feel very good to know we couldn't go along, but then I reckon one boy can't have *all* the fun there is in all the world, and he ought to be glad he gets as much as he does. But I tell you, a red-haired, ruddy-complexioned, seventy-five pound boy can certainly take a lot and still be hungry for more.

I felt a queer lump in my throat when I knew that I couldn't go. For a half minute I was mad at my dad for letting the dentist make that date for me at eight o'clock in the morning. I was also angry at the dentist. Just then, and just before we shut the door and went back into the cabin to wait for Little Jim's dad, I heard

55

from away out in the woods and far up the hill a long, high-pitched dog voice that sounded like a loon and a screaming, trembling hoot owl at the same time, and it was Old Bawler striking a new trail. "*Whoooooooo!*"

Then as if she had called across the valley to Old Sol, we heard him answer, in his long, sad, gruff baritone, "*WHOOOOOOO!*" and we knew another chase was on.

We listened a while, then went inside, shut the door, and began what we supposed would be a very sad half hour waiting for Little Jim's dad to come and get him and the rest of us.

Anyway, I thought, when we were inside and sitting or lying down on the friendly floor beside the fire in the fireplace, *Little Jim can ask about Adam and Eve.* I was getting curious to know the answer myself, mainly I suppose because Little Jim was so anxious to know.

Maybe we could turn on the radio, I thought, and listen to a program. I suggested it to Old Man Paddler. He looked at me and at the rest of us. Then he went over to the radio and was just going to turn it on when we heard steps from somewhere, and I knew it was from the cave entrance to the cabin. Only they were running steps instead of walking like I knew Little Jim's dad's would be, and there wasn't any knock at the wooden door down there in the cellar. Instead, there was something else.

There was a banging and a banging on the door and an excited man's voice calling, "Let me in! Open up and let me in. . . . *Quick!*"

6

"Open up and let me in. . . . Quick!"

Say! Those rough, scared words sounded like—who did they sound like they belonged to?

I looked at Little Jim's mouse-like face, and he was sitting with his fists doubled up. He looked around quick and reached for his stick, which he nearly always carries. It was lying there beside him, a striped stick with half the bark on it and half of it off, making it look like a very long piece of dirty stick candy. He grabbed up that stick and right away looked and probably felt braver.

Dragonfly's dragonfly-like eyes were wide open but still in their sockets. *His* fists were doubled up.

Poetry just looked puzzled, like he had been shocked. I wondered if he was trying to think of a poem and couldn't. Jeep, the picayune, was standing straight up on his four legs, with his short stub of a tail also straight up. He looked like he was going to be very brave. His voice had a deep, gruff growl in it, and he barked a very low, savage bark, which was only a half-bark and a half-growl. The rough brown-tan hair on his back was doing most of his talking for him, and it said "I'm *mad!* I won't let anybody tear anybody's door down without putting up a fight!"

Again there came that rough, scared pounding on the cave door, down the cellar. Old Man Paddler who had been stirring up the fire, turned around quick and said, "Sh! You boys go upstairs. Sh! *Quietly!* I'll handle this. *Hurry,* but no noise!"

I certainly didn't want to go upstairs, not when there was going to be excitement like what I knew there was going to be. That kind voice of Old Man Paddler's had disappeared, and it sounded like he meant business—like my dad's deep voice does sometimes when his bushy eyebrows are down.

As much as I hated to do it, I followed Little Jim and Dragonfly upstairs. And Poetry followed me, none of us being able to do it very quietly.

It was dark up there, but we could see a little by the light from the kerosene lamp which was on the mantle above the table downstairs and also because there was a crack or two in the floor up there.

I could see a lot of things, such as a cot and a bureau and some boxes and a writing desk and an old spinning wheel and different things.

I'd forgotten about the Airedale, but we needn't have worried about him. When he saw us all scrambling up that rough stairway, he must have decided it was a good place to be 'cause there he was, right beside us and right next to Dragonfly. Only he wasn't keeping quiet. I thought maybe I ought to take charge of things up there, so I imagined how Big Jim would have done it, and I said in a harsh whisper to all of us, "Everybody keep quiet, and don't move or whisper, or anything!" It felt good to give orders like that, and for a second I was a general in an army and everybody was obeying me. *ME!* I felt important and as if I was more than I am.

I peeped through the crack in the floor which was right under my eyes. I could see the whole room—the many cups and saucers, not yet washed; the fire crackling in the fireplace; the teakettle on the stove, with steam coming out lazily 'cause it was on the back of the stove; the radio and the map of the world; and Old Man Paddler, with one hand on the iron ring in the trapdoor in the floor, pulling the door up. Then I saw the dark hole which was the cellar, and the wooden steps going down.

"Just a minute!" his voice called down the cellar, and it was very business-like, not a bit scared. It was a different Old Man Paddler than I had ever seen before, and I thought more of him than ever. Just the same, I didn't want him to be alone with what might be a criminal, or he might get hurt. I stayed right close to the stairway and had hold of the other end of Little Jim's stick, just in case the Old Man might need help. It wouldn't take me more than a half-jiffy to get down those steps.

I was trembling though, as bad as Picayune was. I could feel the other end of the stick trembling a little too, and I knew what that meant.

Just then Dragonfly whispered, "Listen!"

I listened, and Dragonfly whispered again, "That's old hook-nosed John Till's voice."

First I heard Seneth Paddler's question as he called from down the cellar, "Who's there?" Then I heard the scared answer, and it was, "It's John Till. Let me in quick. I'm c-cold. I'm nearly frozen."

It was a cold night, but not that cold, I knew. But then he might not have on many clothes.

Anyway, I wasn't as scared as I was before, although John Till and I weren't very good friends. Hadn't been since I'd had a fight with him once in our oats field when he had given Circus's dad some whiskey. I had been so angry that day that I'd jumped in to help Circus in his fight with him and had sunk one of my very hard fists deep into his stomach and had plastered first one and then the other all over his crooked nose for almost four seconds before he had whammed me in the jaw and ended the short fight. I never did forget that.

I lay there, glued fast to the upstairs floor, my eyes watching that trapdoor, my ears grabbing every sound they could. I heard the opening of the wooden cave door, the squeaking of the hinges, and John's voice saying, "Thank you." I was surprised to hear him say that.

A little later, John came up the stairs first, a great big, ugly-looking man, with a crooked nose, and mussed-up hair sticking out under his black felt hat which was pulled down tight onto his forehead. He had a flashlight in his hand which was still on, and he was wearing boots that were muddy and looked like he had been in the swamp down by the sycamore tree. He didn't have on any coat, that is, not any overcoat, so I knew he really was cold. He slumped down into a chair, just as soon as Old Man Paddler had come up and closed the trapdoor, and he stretched his gloveless hands out toward the fire.

The next thing I saw was Old Man Paddler pouring a cup of sassafras tea, first getting a clean cup from the cupboard, and giving the tea with a sandwich to that hungry, trembling man.

He wasn't saying a word, but he kept looking around, afraid of something. I was glad the teakettle was singing a little 'cause we upstairs certainly weren't too quiet. I could hear us breathing and feel my heart beating and the other end of the stick trembling. And I could smell the Airedale who was too close to my nose, and also the sassafras tea from downstairs.

Say, do you know what? Pretty soon, I saw John Till start and jump like he heard something.

"That was a dead branch falling from the old pine tree out there," Seneth Paddler explained. "Have another cup of tea? Here, here's another sandwich left over from— You're probably hungry."

You should have seen that hungry man eat. He almost grabbed the sandwich off the plate the old man handed it to him on.

My own lunch was still down there beside the fireplace. I hadn't eaten it on account of there had been enough other food prepared for us.

Pretty soon Seneth Paddler, who was sitting beside his table, reached up to the mantel piece and took down a black book and laid it close by one of his elbows which was on the table. I knew what kind of book it was, and

60

so did Little Jim who must have seen too 'cause he pressed my arm.

Mr. Paddler's voice was kind again now, since he knew who it was and saw that John Till wasn't going to hurt him.

"Mr. Till," he said, "your son Bob is turning out to be a very respectable boy. We're proud of him, and I know you must too."

Do you know what? I heard a kinda half sob in old hook-nosed John Till's throat as he answered huskily, "Something's changed him, and I guess maybe it's you. You—"

"No, not I," the old voice said, and Seneth Paddler reached out a hand and put it on John Till's shoulder. "It's the power of the—"

I knew exactly what he was going to say, and so did Little Jim and maybe Poetry 'cause they both put their hands on my arm at the same time. I knew the old man was going to say it was an all mighty power, 'cause that was the way he believed, and the way it was. "It's the power of the Lord, John—the same power that will come into your life, too, if you will give Him a chance. There isn't anything too hard for Him."

I couldn't believe my eyes. It *couldn't* be! Not old hook-nosed John Till, I thought. People like him didn't ever change. They just kept on being wicked and mean and then they died and—

Say, Old Man Paddler hadn't any sooner said that than John Till's old black hat came off and he bowed his head and I actually saw several great big tears tumble out and splash down on the rough wooden floor right beside the ring in the trapdoor. All the time, Seneth Paddler's gnarled old hand was on his shoulder.

"Listen, John." I could hear tears in Seneth Paddler's voice, and I knew he not only liked that mean man but even more than that. "Listen, John, I wonder if you will be willing to let me pray for you *right now*.

61

Your two boys ought to have a Christian father, and Mrs. Till has a right to happiness which she'll never have unless—"

John Till shook like he was still cold. That's what Dragonfly thought was wrong when he whispered into my right ear, "He's got a chill, and will maybe get pneumonia."

It wasn't a chill, though.

"Look here," Old Man Paddler said kindly, and there in front of my eyes and right straight in front of John Till's eyes was the old man's open Bible, and he was reading in a voice which still sounded like it had tears in it. This is what we, who were upstairs, actually heard—a part of it anyway, 'cause we couldn't hear very well. It was:

"Whosoever shall call upon the name of the Lord shall be saved."

For a minute I thought I was going to see something. I thought I was going to see hook-nosed John Till bend his rusty knees and actually get right down beside that fireplace and do what the verse in the Bible said for him to.

But say! John Till straightened up, shook his head, pulled out of his hip pocket a red bandana handkerchief and wiped his eyes, blew his nose and said, "Not tonight. No, I can't do it! I ain't goin' to be a coward while the police are after me. I ain't goin' to be weak and turn to religion now."

Right that minute, when old Man Paddler was going to show him another verse, I heard a sound outside. It was a little like a limb falling from a pine tree and a little like something else.

I wondered if it was eleven o'clock and Little Jim's dad had come for us.

John Till must have heard it too, 'cause he jumped, looked up, and his face had a hunted look. He jumped to his feet, looked all around as if trying to see a place to hide, then he saw the stairs and said huskily, "You've been kind to my boy. Now be good to me. Let me hide here tonight, and if they come, you tell 'em I'm not here. Tell them you haven't seen me at all. Tell 'em—"

There was another sound outside like men's voices away out by the spring, coming toward the woodshed and the house. John Till shuffled toward the wooden stairs, and took two or three steps up.

I don't know why on earth I had to sneeze just then or why Jeep had to growl and bark a low, deep, savage growl, but these two things happened.

"Achoo!" I went.

"G-r-r-rrr! Wuff!" went Picayune.

Say! John Till stopped stock still, looked all around, and back into the room, and the next thing we knew he had made a dive for the trapdoor of the cellar, heaved on it, and a second later was down the stairs.

The heavy oak door down there opened and shut with a bang and I heard running footsteps going back into the cave toward the old sycamore tree.

7

Squeak! Bang! Crunch, crunch, crunch-crunch-crunch. That was the way the exit of old hook-nosed John Till sounded to us. It didn't take us long to get downstairs, I tell you. When I reached the bottom of the stairs, Poetry, Little Jim, Dragonfly, and Jeep were all there. In fact Jeep was down there before I was. Old Man Paddler was standing beside the table looking surprised. In his left hand was his black Bible. I think I never saw a man with such a disappointed expression on his face.

"Well, boys," the old man began, then stopped. We looked into his gray eyes and all the twinkle was gone out of them. There was a tremble on his lips which I couldn't see but which I knew was there by the way his long white whiskers were trembling. I don't know why it was I thought that I had heard a sound of voices outside the door because there really hadn't been any there. We opened the door and looked out and called and there wasn't any answer. I guess it was our imagination, mine anyway, that made me think the police were there.

Anyway, I remember that Little Jim's dad had told him that the police were after John Till, and Little Jim had told me that we ought to pray for John Till. And I just had the thing all tangled up in my mind, so that the very minute I heard the sound of falling limbs from the old pine tree outside, I supposed that there were voices.

On the other hand maybe there *were* voices, I don't know. I know one thing and that is, while we were standing there beside and in front of Seneth Paddler, standing, moving and shuffling our nervous feet and looking down the cellar, knowing that John Till had run away, I got to wondering if he might bump into Little

Jim's dad who was supposed to come for us any minute. Maybe the police *were* on his trail and would be waiting for him there at the door and John Till would get caught after all.

I really felt sorry for him.

"Well, boys, I guess we've made a mistake," Old Man Paddler's trembling voice said to us. "We'll have to pray for Bob Till's father." When he said, "Bob's father," I knew that maybe the main reason he wanted John saved was for his boys' sake.

We put the trapdoor down again and sat down in chairs around the fireplace. I opened my lunch pail and divided everything up for everybody and waited for Little Jim's dad to come, not knowing which door he would use. All of a sudden while the five of us were sitting there, Little Jim piped up with the question he'd been wanting to ask for a long time. This is what he said:

"Say, Mr. Paddler, while we were watching the men skin the coon, we got to wondering about the story in the—in the Bible where God made some coats out of the skins of animals and put 'em on Adam and Eve. We wondered why He did that."

Well, sir, Old Man Paddler listened to that little fellow ask that question and I could see right away that he wanted to tell us the correct answer. Nothing made him more happy than for a boy to be interested in things like that. So he smiled—I could tell he was smiling, 'cause the twinkles were in his eyes again—as he sat there on his chair beside the table. He opened his black Bible, turned back to the first part of it, to the book of Genesis, at the right place.

He began to read to us the whole story, and to explain it as he went along, how that Adam and Eve were the very first people there were in the world and that all of us are descended from them.

Dragonfly piped up and said, "I thought the

cavemen were the first people there were in the world."

The old man looked back at him and said over the top of his glasses, "Boys, remember one thing as long as you live. The first man in the world was Adam. As far as that is concerned, there are people *today* in some parts of the world who live in caves. I know, because on my trip around the world I saw some of them. And there are some in some parts of the world—little pigmies, in fact—who still live in *trees,* right in this very world in which all of us live." I knew that was right 'cause it was in one of my schoolbooks.

Then the kind old voice went on and explained it to us. "Maybe I'll never have a chance to tell you boys this again, just like this, but I want you to remember it as long as you live. You all know the story of the cross and of One who was the Son of God, who hung there one day out on a hill called Calvary. You know how out of His veins there flowed the red blood which was His own blood. The Bible says, 'The blood of Jesus Christ, God's Son, cleanseth us all from sin.' "

While Old Man Paddler was telling us that story, I was listening carefully, and it seemed as if I was standing for a minute away back there, outside Jerusalem at the very foot of the hill in front of the cross, looking up toward the blue sky. I could see the face of the Man he was talking about, black and bloody under the hot, thirsty sun. I could see the two thieves, one on either side of Jesus. I could see the heatwaves trembling above the top of the cross like they do on a very sweltering day over the cornfields along Sugar Creek, and the people standing there in their different colored clothes. In my mind I could see the blood flowing out of the wounds in the hands of Jesus and out of the red gashes in His feet where the spikes had been driven in and through and into the wooden cross. I could see the red lifeblood running down the face of the Man when all of a sudden I began to love Him very much because I knew that the Bible said that while He was hanging there, He was dying for the sins of the whole world. And that meant He had done it for *me* and all the Sugar Creek Gang. He had also done it for John Till.

Well, the old man's story went on. Everything was very quiet there in the cabin. All we could hear inside besides the trembling friendly voice, was the crackling of the fire in the fireplace and the sizzle-sizzle of the teakettle. We could hear the wind sighing on the outside of the cabin in the pine trees. My thoughts rambled around a little. Getting all mixed up with the sound of the fire and the wind in the trees and the teakettle, it seemed as if I could hear the *crunch, crunch, crunch, crunch-crunch-crunch* of John Till's shoes as they hurried away down the cave. Then for a minute it seemed as if I could hear the footsteps of one of Jesus' disciples, a man whose name was Judas, and how when he realized he had betrayed Him, he ran away to hang himself. I could sorta hear his footsteps also, as they went *crunch-crunch-crunch*, as he hurried away out through the suburbs of the city to the place where he was going to find a maple or maybe an olive tree to hang himself on, there not being any maple trees over where he lived.

Crunch, crunch, crunch . . . crunch-crunch-crunch . . . until their sound disappeared.

Then the story the old man was telling made my mind swing back clear across thousands of years to the first two people there were in the world again, and I was standing in a very beautiful park-like garden listening.

I didn't expect Little Jim to pipe up and interrupt him right then, but he did it so quick that I was surprised when he asked, "Did He do it for Adam and Eve so they'd have a cover for their—for their *sins*, maybe?"

The old man who had been talking with his glasses on so he could read when he wanted to, looked up at all

68

of us, took off his glasses so he could see us better, and then guessing maybe which one of us had asked the question said, "That's right, Little Jim, until someday His only Son came to take them all *away*."

It was the easiest thing in the world to listen to that story. It was a little bit too long for me to tell all over again for you, but somehow I was glad a man like John Till (or even Bill Collins) had Someone on his trail, tracking him everywhere he went—not to hurt or kill him but to *save* him.

I was glad all those people back there a long time ago had had an object lesson so it would be easy for them to understand that someday there would be a real Savior. . . .

Well, it was a great story, as I said, and little bit too long and hard for me to remember what the kind, friendly, white-whiskered old man said, but we listened to it, and we understood. And I wished Old John Till had heard it. I wished all the people in the world could understand about it. I wished that the heathen in America and in other countries could hear it.

Little Jim piped up and said, "What are all those colored pins over there on the map for?"

Old Man Paddler stood up, then sat down, and began to talk about the map of the world. "Well, boys," he began, "it's a little secret which I haven't told anybody about. I wanted all the Sugar Creek Gang to be here at the same time to hear about it, but I can tell you tonight, anyway."

Do you know what that man had on that map? He had a pin on it for every missionary he was praying for—a yellow pin for missionaries in China, the black-headed ones for those who were missionaries to Africans, the light-brown for those who were missionaries to people who were light-brown-white people, such as many who lived in Mexico and South America and Cuba. . . .

All of a sudden, I remembered what I was supposed to say to Old Man Paddler, so I said, "Say, my dad said for me to remember to tell you that he was coming up to see you tomorrow to talk to you about Cuba."

That old man sighed, smiled, stood up, and walked over beside the map, like a teacher in a schoolroom. He pointed with one of his long, bony fingers at the caterpillar-shaped island of Cuba, and he said, "Boys, I want you to keep your eyes on that place, look it up in your geography and history books and in other books such as encyclopedias, and be ready for action. I have a surprise for you one of these days."

That's all the old man said, but there was a mysterious something in his voice that made me feel good.

"What kind of surprise?" fat Poetry beside me asked courteously. Poetry had a very serious look on his face 'cause at home he had a scrapbook in which he kept pictures of missionaries and maps of things telling about them, his parents being especially glad he wasn't making a scrapbook of movie stars and things like that. For all his mischievousness, Poetry had a good mind that could think serious things, even though you couldn't always tell it.

"Well," again there was a mysterious something in the trembling old voice. He said, "Boys, how would you like to go down there some of these days?"

I suddenly felt my heart leap and start off on a fast race like it was going somewhere itself. I remembered that that kind old man had sent us on a camping trip up North and paid all of our expenses just because he liked boys so well and because he wanted us to learn a lot of first aid things and camp life and about the New Testament, which his nephew, Barry Boyland, had taught us on that trip. I knew also that Old Man Paddler had spent some of his money to send the whole Sugar Creek

70

Gang to Chicago, and we'd had a wonderful time. And I knew also that he had a lot of money that he wasn't wasting on himself but that he was willing to spend on different people, so do you know what I got to wondering? I got to thinking that maybe that generous-hearted old man had planned somehow or other that the Sugar Creek Gang would all get to go across the southeast corner of the United States and down the east coast of Florida. Maybe, well, maybe we'd get on a boat or an airplane or something and go away over one hundred and thirty miles across the ocean to that beautiful little island of Cuba which is one of the islands that Columbus discovered. Poetry said that Columbus said it was the most beautiful island in the world.

I wished it and I wished it and I wished it.

Pretty soon it was eleven o'clock and time for Little Jim's dad to come for us. Then I heard a sound of steps on the twigs outside and a knock on the front door and it was the one I thought it was.

Little Jim's dad, as you know, was the township trustee and had to look after boys who played truant, and such things as that. He was a fine person, whom all of us liked very much. He is the one who was especially kind to Big Bob Till, John's oldest boy, and he was the one to whom the government had paroled Bob. He came in, and we all got ready to go home. Old Man Paddler let us go down to his cellar to take the short cut to the sycamore tree to save a lot of walking, although eight o'clock in the morning would come just as quick no matter how long it took us to get home.

We opened the solid oak door in the cellar. With our flashlights and with Jeep, the picayune, we started to walk through to the tree at the mouth of the cave.

It looked as if our fun for the whole evening was over, so we started telling Little Jim's dad about John Till and all the different things that had happened.

"We caught a possum all by ourselves," Dragonfly

71

said. "Jeep treed him and Circus climbed the tree and—"

"Jeep got onto a *sidetrack*," Poetry said, going on with the story from where he had made Dragonfly leave off, "and there happened to be a possum close by, which looked like it wouldn't hurt a picayune, so he ran away from the coon and chased the helpless possum up a persimmon tree."

That was the way we all felt—happy and cheerful. All except Bill Collins who wondered how *many* teeth would have to be filled and who wished he had drunk more milk the past year or two and not had so much candy or his teeth would have been better.

Right away almost we came to the canvas at the mouth of the cave, pushed it aside, and stepped out into the world again. And there we were by the side of the lightning-gashed sycamore tree. We hadn't any sooner stepped out than, do you know, Jeep, the picayune, pricked up his queer-looking ears and acted like he was hearing something. Then he sniffed his nose into the air and acted like he was smelling something. Then he looked, swung his head around, and looked straight ahead of where his nose was pointing, away out into the dark like he was seeing something. I looked at him all over, and the rough, brown and light-brown curly hair on his back started to move and stand up a little.

He began to growl first, then to bark in his throat. Then like a shot he swished out through the woods as fast as he could go toward the path that leads through the swamp. Away out there somewhere he started in to barking fiercely like he had something treed or else like there was a rabbit in a brushpile or something.

Dragonfly, standing beside me, raised his excited voice and yelled, "Come back here, Jeep. You crazy picayune! Leave that rabbit alone!"

Say, that little Airedale had a strange sound in his nervous voice. He didn't sound like he was barking at a rabbit, but at something he'd never seen before, something very important!

"Jeep!" Dragonfly cried again, but his voice was swallowed up by Jeep's yelping and barking, as if that tan dog was begging us to come and see what he had caught or was about to catch.

So, out we went, Little Jim's dad leading the way at first. Then because I knew the swamp better than he did, he let me lead the way and the rest followed me. I had a long flashlight in my hand. I knew just where to walk and not get off the trail into the slime and ooze.

Just then my flashlight showed me where Jeep was, behind a wild rosebush, and he was barking more excitedly than ever. In a jiffy we were all there.

Then I let out a scream which I certainly didn't intend to, but couldn't help it 'cause I saw SOMETHING!

SOMETHING, I tell you! "Look!" I cried, and every nerve was trembling so much I dropped the flashlight, and of course nobody could see till I'd picked it up again. I was so weak and scared, I couldn't even call loud. But I held the flashlight out toward the place again, past the barking, panting dog, and saw it again.

"Look! Everybody. Look! There's a—there's a man's head lying out there all by itself!"

8

I had never seen anything like that before in all my life—a man's head lying out in the middle of the swamp. My flashlight was straight on it, and I could see the eyes blinking and the lips moving. And then I heard a voice call loud and frightened, "Help! *H-E-L-P!*"

Well, what would you do if you saw somebody's head lying out in a swamp, and you heard a voice calling, "He-e-e-e-elp," and the voice sounded worse than Old Bawler's long sad high voice trembling across the woods?

"*HELP . . . HELP . . . !*"

Dragonfly saw it, too, and he was more excited than ever. The dog was barking. Poetry was talking. Little Jim's dad was talking. Dragonfly's voice broke in then and he cried, "It's John Till! It's old hook-nosed John Till. He's got off the path that leads through the swamp and has stepped off into the quagmire, and he's going down. We've got to save him!"

I tell you it looked like we ought to do something and we ought to do it mighty quick! I looked at that little barking Airedale, who looked up and back at us, with a worried expression on his face, and at the same time he seemed to be saying, "I told you I wasn't any picayune! I told you I wasn't an insignficiant person or thing!"

Well, not only did we see old hook-nosed John Till's head lying out there in the swamp—that is, that's what it looked like at first—but I knew he had done what Dragonfly said. He had stepped aside from the path and there he was floundering around in the quicksand, and the quicksand had slipped from under his feet and he had gone down, down, down until he was all the way down to his neck. Then I saw his hands were out and he was holding them out kinda like a little baby holds out its hands—like my baby sister, Charlotte Ann, holds out her hands to my mom when she is in her bassinet and wants to get out and can't and feels terribly unhappy about something. She reaches up to my mom to reach down her nice kind arms and pull her out and up.

We knew it wasn't safe for any of us to get any nearer than Jeep himself was, so the only thing we could do for a minute was to stand there and argue with ourselves on the inside to decide what to do.

Little Jim's dad said, "We ought to have a rope. We ought to have a tree or sapling or something to push out to him so he can catch hold of it."

None of us had any ax or hatchet with us, and we knew we wouldn't have time to take our knives and cut down a small tree and trim all the small branches off, and push it out to hook-nosed John Till so he could catch hold of it. All the time he was hollering for help 'cause he was not only in clear up to his neck, but he was down so far that he had to keep his chin lifted or he couldn't even breathe.

We knew that most any minute he would slip down under and that would be the end. He was struggling like a boy who is trying to swim and keep himself up above the water and can't 'cause he has cramps. I tell you my mind got to working quick. My brain generally works quicker when I am angry about something, but it started to work quick right that minute too when I realized that something ought to be done to save that man's life. I was thinking what if he'd actually gone on down there and his mouth would get filled with that awful quicksand and he would actually smother and choke to death and he would have to leave his body and go up into eternity somewhere to meet God. He would be lost forever on account of him being stubborn and rebellious and not willing to bow his stubborn old will and confess that he was an honest-to-goodness sinner needing a Savior—the only One there is. And you know what His Name is.

I felt sorry for Little Tom Till, and for his big brother, Big Bob Till, and how they would miss their dad even if he was mean to them. I felt sorry especially for the boys' mother, Mrs. Till with her sad face, who had a hard enough time to make a living as it was, although it would be easier for her if John Till was dead, and then—well, if he was dead and didn't spend all the money he earned on himself. I even remembered that sometimes my mom let Mrs. Till do our washing and paid her more than it was worth, so as to be kind to her.

Say, Old John Till spend most of his money and his time in the combination pool hall and beer parlor in our town, and you never saw him in church. Not *once!*

"Here," Poetry said, "here's something that we could get out to him if we could get it." In a jiffy he had slipped his hand into his pocket and out again with his knife. He opened the blade while I held the flashlight for him, and in only a second he had a grapevine cut in two at its root. You see all around Sugar Creek and especially around the swamp and down along the old bayou where we played, there were grapevines that came up out of the ground not very far from trees, and they sometimes grew up beside the trees, holding onto the trees, and then on up into the branches. In some places the grapevines were so long that they reached clear up into the tops of the trees. Well, I knew that that was an idea. The only thing was we'd have to have a vine that was about fifteen or twenty feet long or longer in order to save that man out there.

Of course if we had wanted to, we might have made a rope out of ourselves or a ladder or something. I could have lain down on the ground—or Poetry could have—and I could have lain down at the end of his big feet and taken hold of them, and Dragonfly could have crawled out beyond me and held onto my feet. But that wouldn't have made a very strong rope, and we might have lost a boy as well as John Till.

Just a second I hesitated wishing Circus was there to go shinning up that red oak tree 'cause he could have done it quick as a monkey and could have cut the vine off up there and then we could have thrown it out to John Till in time to save his life. I thought all these things in less than even a jiffy. Then I did some quick acting, for me, much quicker than I do when my dad tells me to do something I don't especially want to do and should.

I didn't have time to think any more 'cause I was already on my way up that rough-barked oak tree. I was up there right away, which is terribly quick, and what do you suppose? I held on as tight as I could, wrapping my legs around the tree to keep from falling, and shoved one hand into my pocket to get hold of my knife. I didn't have it.

All the time Jim Till was hollering for help. All the time Picayune was barking, first at me up the tree, and then at John Till and then at the excitement, and all the time I was wishing I would hurry and I couldn't. It was like being in a dream, in which you are trying to run away from a mad bull and can't even run. I was just standing—*hanging* there, holding on.

Poetry yelled up to me, "You can have *my* knife!"

He started to throw it up to me, and he did. It came sizzling up through the air but I couldn't see it, and it came down in the leaves beside the footpath and was lost. Say, Little Jim's dad sprang into action. He had his knife in his hand, his own, and right away he was on his way up the tree to where I was, and he was almost as good a climber as Circus. He had his knife out of his pocket quick. He handed it to me and before you could say Jack Robinson Crusoe, I had that vine in two.

Little Jim's dad slid down that tree and in less than almost no time at all he had the other end of the vine out to where John Till was. He was not a bit deeper down, as if maybe he had managed to stay up by struggling.

Talk about a drowning man clinging to a straw! Old hook-nosed John Till hooked his long fingers around that end of the vine, and we started to pull, all of us that could get hold of our end—that is, I did as soon as I was down the tree.

It looked good to see John slowly coming up a little and toward the safe place where we were. I was glad. Then suddenly, somebody hollered, "Hey! Hey! Where's Little Jim! He's *g-gone!*"

John Till was sliding back into the quicksand again, it seemed, for Poetry's yell unnerved us all so that for a second we forgot what we were doing.

Little Jim GONE! My head swam round and round and round. What on *earth* had happened! Had he slipped away while we weren't watching, or had he tried to go out there and get John Till and had slid down in himself?

I guess the excitement made us pull too hard on the grapevine then 'cause the very worst thing that could have happened *did* happen, and that was—well, I *heard* it before I could believe it. I *felt* it next, and then I *knew* it 'cause all of a sudden I lost my balance and stumbled backward over Dragonfly and Mr. Foote's foot, and we all landed in a heap on top of and underneath each other *'cause the grapevine rope had broken!*

9

It's a terrible feeling knowing you have to save a man's life or it will never be saved—knowing that if you don't do something, nothing will be done.

It's a worse feeling when all of a sudden while you're saving the life of a man you don't like very well, you discover your best friend is gone and you don't know where and you think maybe you'll never see him again.

There we were with our broken vine, all in a tumbled jumble of legs and arms and bodies and with a dog barking excitedly so we couldn't think straight and with everything upside down including ourselves, trying to think what to do next, anyway trying to *think,* when from behind us I heard the sweetest music I'd ever heard in most of my life. It was Little Jim's voice. He was saying, "Here, Daddy! Here's one of the canvas curtains from the cave. We can make a rope out of that."

I felt so good that I jumped to my feet, whirled around, and made a dive for Little Jim and the canvas. I knew we'd have to cut it into strips and tie the strips together, twisting them so the new rope would be strong enough not to break.

I whirled around so quick that I lost my balance and stepped too far to one side of our safe place, and the next thing I knew I was out in the ooze and water and mud. It looked like I was in the quicksand. I began to go down, down, down, feeling like there was a suction down there pulling on the bottom of my boots. Right away I was halfway down to the top of my high boots, so I began to scream for help myself.

Poetry, who was standing closest to me, reached out his fat hand. I caught hold of it and managed to pull one of my feet out. It made a sucking noise like an old cow's foot does when she pulls it out of about ten inches of mud in a very muddy barnyard. Almost right away I was back onto solid ground again, and I knew we didn't dare trifle with danger. It would be very easy for every single one of us to get out there and every single one of us would go down.

It didn't take Little Jim's dad very long to get a makeshift rope made out of that tough canvas.

We tossed one end out to where John Till could get hold of it.

"Hey!" I yelled out to him. "Don't pull so *hard*!" For he was pulling and pulling like he was half scared to death, and maybe he was.

Hand over hand, every one of us pulled as carefully as he could, that is, Little Jim's dad and Poetry were pulling, and they had a good strong grip.

Steadily, steadily, we saw that man come up out of the mire. When we got him a little closer, he found solid ground under his feet. He was about waist deep at the time, right where I had been a little while before, so I knew I couldn't have gone *clear* down.

I tell you while I was holding that flashlight so everybody could see, I saw the strangest person I ever saw. Absolutely covered with mud, a whitish, brownish, yellowish, mud or clay or quicksand or whatever it was, from his chin clear down to the toes of his boots. He must have been very cold for he was trembling and trembling and scared, and all of a sudden I remembered a story which I'd once read somewhere. A jail keeper was doing the same thing—trembling. He sprang out of the jail door and said to Paul and Silas, the Christian men who had been staying in his jail 'cause they had preached the gospel—he said to them, "What must I do to be saved?" That's a very important question which anybody can answer by saying what Paul said to that scared jailer and that was, "Believe on the Lord Jesus Christ, and thou shalt be saved, and thy house," meaning your whole family can be saved the same way. But Paul wasn't talking about being saved from the quicksand but about being saved *forever* and having eternal life.

I didn't get to think anymore along that line. John Till was standing there trembling, so we knew we had to do something. Little Jim's dad said, "Well, John, your life has been saved. If you'll come along home with me we'll get you some clean, dry clothes."

John Till stood still. There was a sob in his voice like he'd had in the cabin. He said, "Mr. Foote, I made up my mind while I was down there going down deeper calling for help and nobody heard me, I made up my mind that—that I was goin' to go straight. I made up my mind I wasn't goin' to live the kind of life I'd lived all these years. Made up my mind I was goin' to go to church. Made up my mind—"

He just stood there and shook and sobbed and some more tears came out. One of them fell right down on his muddy right hand, the very same hand that last summer had been all doubled up into a fist and had whammed me on the jaw and knocked the daylights out of me. . . .

"Made up my mind," he went on with his voice choking, "that I was goin' to set an example for my boys. I was goin' to follow Jesus. I was goin' to be a good man, was goin' to follow Him to heaven."

Do you know that was a wonderful thing? I guess I felt pretty good to hear a bad man say that. But I was surprised to hear Little Jim's dad say, "That's wonderful, John. You know there are going to be a lot of people at Sugar Creek happy because of that. But do you know, John, that that won't save you?"

We all started then toward the Footes' house 'cause

John Till was so cold. We took a shortcut through the woods and all the way home, Little Jim's dad explained things to John.

You could hear our boots squishing squashing. You could hear John Till's boots doing the same thing 'cause they were full of water. It was pitiful to look at him with the mud all over him like that. I hoped the police wouldn't come and get him. I hoped he was really meaning business this time, that he was actually going to do what he said he was going to do.

One of the things Little Jim's dad said was, "That won't save you, John. You couldn't follow the example of Jesus and be saved that way."

All the rest of us were listening, not understanding it very well, but knowing enough to keep still. "It's this way, John," Little Jim's dad said. "Suppose while you were down there in the quagmire all the way up to your chin that I had stood there on the safe solid ground and said to you, 'Look at me, John Till! Turn over a new leaf! Just follow me and I'll take you home! See how tall and straight I am. See how I stand on this solid ground! Look at me and follow me along home!' "

John Till didn't say anything for maybe twenty-five feet of walking. All we could hear was the squishing and the crunching and the other noises our shoes and boots made as we hurried through the woods. We could hear the wet leaves scrunching under our feet. Now and then in a dry place we could hear the rattle of the dry ones, which reminded Poetry of a poem which we had in our school books. We were far enough behind to listen to him quote it without disturbing Mr. Foote and John Till, so Poetry quoted a part of it:

> . . . the husky rusty, rustle
> Of the tassels of the corn . . .

Then we listened again to the men, and Mr. Foote

was saying, "If I'd told you *that,* you'd have thought I was crazy. You see, you had to be *saved first,* and *then* you could follow me home."

Hearing that was just like turning on a small light in my mind. It was as clear as broad daylight on a summer day exactly how to be saved. If anybody wanted to be saved and go to heaven and follow Jesus home, he never could do it until after he had been rescued. First he had to be lifted out of a quagmire. I was explaining it to Little Jim the best I could, and I said to him, "You have to be lifted out of the quagmire of—" I kinda hated to say the word which is spelled s-i-n, even though it was a Bible word and everybody was a sinner. Little Jim piped across the top of a small rosebush to me, and said, "First you have to be saved from sin, and then you can follow Jesus." And I knew that little fellow had said the truth.

Well, we could see the light in Little Jim's dad's house, and we could see Little Jim's mom sitting beside their radio. We knew that pretty soon we would be there.

I say I saw Little Jim's mom sitting by the radio. I couldn't really tell, except that I knew their radio was standing near their window. About that minute we came to a rail fence. All of us climbed over and down into a deep side ditch, scrambled up through the long, tangled-up dead weeds, which in the summertime had been very green along the fence row there, and reached the narrow lane, or road, that goes right up to Little Jim's house and on past to the little red-brick schoolhouse where all the Sagar Creek Gang goes to school.

There was a little hill which we had to climb before we came to the front gate. Mr. Foote opened the gate and we were about ready to go in, when we saw the lights of a car come swinging down the road—*up* the road, rather, where we had just been. The car was going very fast. It went bangety-bang across the little wooden bridge which spans the small tributary that flows into Sugar Creek. When the car reached the lane that leads into the Footes' barnyard, it swung in and stopped all of a sudden, and a powerful, bright search-light swung around over in our direction and lighted up every one of us.

You could see us as plain as day, standing there by the narrow wooden gate just getting ready to go through.

"It's the police!" Poetry whispered harshly to me.

You know, I expected John Till to get scared again and turn around and hurry away. I thought he'd run down the little road and dive under the bridge. But do you know what? John Till said, "It's—it's the police, and they're after me. It's all right. I'm ready to go. I'm ready to go!"

It was just as if he had heard the policemen in the car over there telling him to put his hands up 'cause he didn't wait. He shot both mud-covered hands right up in the air, swung back through the small gate, and started walking toward the light. He raised his voice and called to them, "I'm surrendering!"

A policeman stepped out of the car, walked over toward him, snapped on a pair of handcuffs, and was going to make him get into the car. Little Jim's dad spoke up then and said, "Men, John Till is ready to surrender to you, and he is willing to go to jail tonight, but he's been out in the swamp and he's all covered with mud. I'd like to take him into our house and let him have a good warm bath, a lunch, and a change of clothes. I have a suit that he could wear, and then I'll bring him down to the jail to you as soon as he is ready, or I'll bring him down tomorrow morning. He can stay at our house all night if he wants to."

Say, I knew that *Bob* Till was already living there 'cause he was paroled to Mr. Foote, and I started to wonder something but didn't get to finish it.

Well, most policemen are kind when they have to arrest people, even though they have to be very firm sometimes. Anyway this one said, "He won't need to take any bath first. We have a shower down at the jail. And as for clothes, we have a striped suit down there which he can wear. John Till," he said as he directed his words to trembling, very cold, and quiet John Till, "climb into the back of the car there!" That voice was kind but it meant business.

Mr. Till hesitated a minute. He looked over at Little Jim's dad. Then he looked around the circle at the rest of us, and in a very trembling voice—maybe trembling because he was still so cold or 'cause he was still not over being frightened—he said, "Boys, I've never had any use for the Sugar Creek Gang up to this time, but you've proved to me that you are gentlemen. I'm proud to have my son Tom be a member of your gang. I'm proud of the way you've treated my boy Bob. And now I'm proud of the way you have treated me. I'm not goin' to forget it in a long time. I want to thank you.

"And now—" John Till was still talking. He stopped in a very short jiffy. I could hear the rattle of the handcuffs on his wrists. I don't think I ever felt so very sorry for a man in my life before. I hated to see him have to have the punishment he deserved, and yet there wasn't anything any of us could do about it. Just that minute—I guess it had been clearing up all the time—the weather, I mean—anyway, I was surprised when the moon came bursting out from under a bank of clouds and shone down through the woods and through the leafless trees in the yard there and on John Till's face. For some reason, I decided I liked John Till and was going to be kind to him. So I started to say something, but the words got stuck in my throat. I sounded like a frog's voice does when he is trying to

87

holler in the spring along the creek and his voice chokes off and he sounds like a tin can that has been hit by a rock which some boy has thrown at it.

I did say, though, "John Till—" My voice sounded like the tin can again, but I stayed with it until I had said, "Mr. Till, Little Tom is one of my best friends. I like him very m-much."

Then the gruff-voiced policeman said, "All right, John Till! We'll can the sob stuff. Into the backseat there!"

John turned. There wasn't anything we could do, not a thing. We just had to stand there and watch him get in, listen to the car door slam, hear the motor speed up as the driver stepped on his accelerator, and then watch the big black car as it backed out of the drive and swung around backing a little way toward the Sugar Creek schoolhouse. Then we watched it as it went forward and down the hill, across the little tributary bridge, and on up the hill on the other side of the valley. Pretty soon its two taillights looked like two tiny red stars up at the top of the hill.

John Till was on his way to jail.

I didn't know till later that the reason John Till hadn't gone down *clear under* was because when he got down up to his neck, his foot had struck a rock down there, and he'd been balancing himself on it. If his foot had slipped off while we were taking such a long time rescuing him, he'd have gone down for sure.

10

Yes, John Till was on his way to jail; and in a few minutes the Sugar Creek Gang—all there were with us at the time—were on our way home in Little Jim's dad's automobile.

Not only that, but this Sugar Creek Gang story is on the way to end. It won't be long now until I shall come to the very last word.

All the time as I rode along in Little Jim's dad's kinda half-oldish car I kept thinking about what my dad was going to say to Seneth Paddler when he called to see him the next day in his rustic old cabin in the hills. You know, I could see in my mind's eye that little log cabin with its clapboard roof, with its backdoor down in the basement. I could see the old flintlock on the wall. I could see the little cow's horn with a cap on the large end, which had been used for powder a long time ago. I could see the clean-looking bed. I could see the stairway.

I kept thinking about it as we all rode along. Little Jim riding along with us 'cause his dad said he could if he wanted to. Dragonfly and Poetry rode along in the backseat 'cause they lived in the same direction as I did. We went across the noisy little bridge that spanned the tributary and then on following the same trail that the police car had when its two red taillights had looked like two crimson stars up at the top of the hill, on farther and farther up that little lane-like road until we came to the cornfields across from our house.

We turned left pretty soon at a great, tall, branching elm tree, which in the summertime had enough shade for many boys to play in. But we hardly ever played there. It wasn't a very friendly tree for its branches were so very high. Its bole was too large around for any of us boys to climb. Not even Circus had ever climbed it and didn't even want to. Every other tree along Suagar Creek seemed to belong to us and maybe had grown just for us but this one didn't seem to belong.

We turned there, drove along the end of my dad's last year's cornfield, turned again in a little while, and went left down the road to the Collins' house. As I sat there in the front seat with Little Jim in between me and his dad looking down the graveled road to our house, I could see a light in the kitchen window. I knew that my mom and my dad would be awake waiting for me, and I could hardly wait to tell them everything that had happened.

I tell you there is something grand about coming home, something grand. Pretty soon, Mr. Foote's car swung in and stopped beside our front gate, not very far from the mail box which had printed on it the words THEODORE COLLINS, which is my dad's name. The car lights shone on those letters, and I felt proud of my great big dad. I climbed out of the car and said, "Good night, Mr.—Mr. Foote. Thank you very, very much." Little Jim was all slumped over beside his daddy. He was so sleepy. Poetry and Dragonfly in the backseat were still pretty wide awake, although I could tell by looking close into Dragonfly's dragonfly-like eyes that he was getting very, very drowsy.

For a minute I forgot all about having to have my teeth filled in just a little while. I said, "So long, everybody." Then I turned and lifted up the little latch that let me into our front gate. Dad had shut it like he always does at night. I walked across the only footpath my folks will let me have across our yard, on account of Mom wanting a nice grassy lawn, and came to the boardwalk that leads from our back porch steps to the pitcher pump maybe twenty feet away. I lifted up the pump handle a minute, listened to it squeak as I shoved it down, and watched a nice stream of water come spouting out, sparkling in the moonlight. I watched the pretty little ripples it made in the tub out of which our horses drink sometimes. Sometimes Old Mixy herself drinks out of that tub.

I started toward the back porch steps. Then I stopped for a minute and looked back up toward the moon which was sailing in a very pretty sky, and I thought about all the things I had been thinking about. Somehow or other as I looked at that great, big, beautiful, half-round moon with what looked like continents of different shapes on it, I thought about it being the same moon that would be shining on Old Man Paddler's cabin, the same moon that would be shining on the jail where John Till was right that minute taking a shower bath. And then, looking at those dark places on the moon that looked like islands or continents on a globe, I got to thinking it would be the same moon that would be shining down upon that little caterpillar-shaped island, away down around the northern part of the Caribbean Sea. I got to thinking how nice it would be if I could go sailing up in an airplane, away up in the sky above the clouds under a moon like that with the ocean down below and with the whole Sugar Creek Gang sitting in the seats all around me.

I tell you it felt good to imagine having a ride like that. Pretty soon I heard the door latch of our backdoor squeak. Then I heard the door latch open with the same noise it always makes. Then the screen door opened and there was the same friendly squeaking in its springs. My dad's great big voice that nearly always sounds deep like a bull frog's voice does along Sugar Creek was calling to me and said:

"Well, Bill Collins! Come on into the house."

He said it so cheerfully. I looked up at my dad and there he was with his big striped pajamas on. I was glad to see him. I could see our lamp lit, standing on the shelf there on the mantel. just as I came in the door and had it shut, I heard my mom call from the bedroom away on the other side of the living room. "Well," she said, "my boy is home again. Did you have a nice time? *No!*" She raised her voice a little to say that and then added, "Don't tell me now, I'm too sleepy. Wait till morning to tell us."

Well sir, the way she said that made me want to start in and tell her everything that happened on our hunting trip. So I started in and was almost immediately interrupted by my dad with, "Say, Bill Collins, it's after midnight! You'll have to hurry or you won't get any sleep before the dentist starts grinding on your teeth at ten o-clock tomorrow morning!"

Wham! That was the way it felt to have him remind me of tomorrow morning at eight. "What!" I said. "What time did you say?"

My dad's deep voice laughed as he said, "Just after you left I called Dr. Mellen and told him that eight o'clock would be a bit early for you on Saturday if you were up late Friday night. So he looked over his appointments and telephoned back a little later. He said he'd had a cancellation. He said John Till was to come in at ten, but he didn't think he would be there, so—"

Say, that started me in to talking 'cause I felt so good to think I didn't have to get up so early, and even Mom felt better about it. Before I was through, I had talked and talked and talked. I had to wait till morning for some of it though 'cause they didn't want me to wake up Charlotte Ann by mimicking the hounds and Jeep, which I had been doing every now and then in my story.

In the morning, though, which was a wonderful morning, I finished all the things I hadn't thought of the night before. By the time I was through I had told my parents everything which you have already read.

Then Dad took me to the dentist's office. "How

long will it take?" he asked Dr. Mellen who right that minute had me in the big chair with my mouth open and a small mirror with a handle on it moving it around beside my teeth just before he started grinding.

Dr. Mellen looked at his wristwatch and said, "Not long. Maybe thirty minutes."

"I'll wait," Dad said. And then he said to me, "You can go with me to see Old Man Paddler if you want to."

And I wanted to. I tell you, if we get to go to a foreign country because Old Man Paddler sends us there, it'll be the first time in my life I've ever been out of the United States. Also the first time I've been in an airplane above the ocean.